Praise for Shattered Rules

What Readers Say:

"Shattered Rules, an excellent book - I loved this!!!"

"Intense!!! Kept me on the edge of my seat the entire time!"

"Wow — one of the most exciting and suspenseful stories I've read in a long time! Incredibly intense, this had me on the edge of my seat the entire time. I could not put this book down! Filled with action, escalating tension, danger, death threats, spies, the FBI, twists, turns, betrayal, and love. Amazing story — this is well written and powerful."

"An exciting, intense, mystery!"

"An enthralling read that takes you in from the first sentence."

"Excellent book - I loved this! This was my favorite, edge-of-your-seat book this year! Very exciting with increasing tension throughout! Highly recommended!"

"A non-stop suspense from the first chapter until the end!"

I0637951

Dedication

To Lee Lee, who knew I could.

To the unsung heroes who decide, even under extraordinary circumstances, to do the right thing.

Acknowledgments

Thank you to my great critique partners!

About the author

Reggi Allder writes suspense and contemporary novels. Her characters must overcome obstacles in both genres, as in real life. The males are strong, though they may be wounded. The women are determined to change their lives to manage their future. They fight to discover a hidden strength and work toward a lifelong goal.

She studied creative writing and screenwriting at the University of California at Los Angeles (UCLA). Besides the standalone books, she writes The Sierra Creek Series, Book One is Her Country Heart, and the Dangerous Series, Book One is Dangerous Web. She has also contributed to cookbooks and has written children's stories.

Reggi enjoys hearing from readers. Follow her on Bookbub.com, and Facebook.

Shattered Rules

Can you keep a secret?

Reggi Allder

Books by Reggi Allder

Suspense
Shattered Rules
Dangerous Series
Dangerous Web
Dangerous Denial
Dangerous Money
Dangerous Moves

Contemporary
Sierra Creek Series
Her Country Heart
His Country Heart
Our Country Heart
My Country Heart
Her Country Heart Christmas Edition

Historical
With Glowing Hearts

Coming Next
Dangerous Sisters

Chapter 1

The sound of the doorbell broke the late-night silence. Kelly Shaw woke with a start, sat up in bed, and squinted to see the alarm clock. Eleven forty-five.

The bell buzzed again.

Out of bed, she adjusted her short blue cotton nightgown and rushed to the bedroom window. A brown delivery van idled in the dimly lit driveway. Maybe the airline had finally found her sister's lost suitcase. She threw on her robe and ran from the room.

In the foyer, she flipped on the overhead porch light and peered out the sidelight window. A tall man in a brown uniform smiled at her.

"You're working late," she shouted through the glass.

"You're the last delivery."

"Leave it on the porch."

"I need a signature."

"Okay."

When the tumblers on the deadbolt lock turned, the front door flew open and the man lunged at her, slamming her against the foyer wall. Before she could scream, the intruder grabbed her by the throat.

"Yell and you're dead."

She held her hand tightly against her mouth to push back a scream.

A smaller man rushed into the house and jogged down the hall toward the kitchen.

The man holding her loosened his grasp.

"Get out," she whispered. "Get out of my house."

"Shut up."

"What do you want?"

Muscular, with black hair and a tanned complexion, the stranger glared at her. "Where the hell is it?"

"Where is what?"

"Wrong answer." He twisted her arm. "Tell me."

She whimpered.

With a smile, he yanked her to him. His body heat burned through her thin cotton robe. She coughed as warm cigarette breath played across her face. His black eyes gazed downward and gawked at her breasts.

Fear pulsed in her.

The sound of slamming cupboard doors and breaking glass came from the kitchen.

The smaller man poked his head out of the kitchen doorway. The odor of French coffee beans and Italian spices wafted from the room. "Nothing in there." He ran down the hall toward the bedrooms.

The stranger yanked her into the hallway.

If she could break free, she'd run out the front door.

As if he heard her thinking, he tightened his grip.

She screamed.

He slapped her. "If you don't keep quiet I'll kill you now."

Now? Did that mean he was going to kill her later? She closed her eyes. *Don't panic. Don't panic.*

He pushed her forward.

She stumbled into her bedroom and gasped as her mattress was thrown against the wall by the smaller man. He pulled out a switchblade knife, slit it open, and ripped out the stuffing. Then he jerked open the dresser drawers and dumped the contents onto the beige pile carpet.

Liquid dripped from an open perfume bottle and the fragrance of roses filled the room.

The clothes from her closet were tossed onto the bedroom floor.

2

Shattered Rules

The intruder held the knife to her neck. "Give it to me or I'll cut you."

She trembled, afraid to speak with the knife at her throat.

"I could slit your gullet and bury your body. No one would be the wiser." He moved the knife from her neck.

She gulped for air.

He pushed her from him, then ripped a photograph of her late father off the wall. He looked inside the frame and tossed it and the photo onto the floor, crushing it under his booted feet.

"No." She grabbed the mangled photo and held it to her.

He seized her with one hand. With the other, he rifled through her things.

Johnny Vega must have sent these guys. She shouldn't have come home tonight.

Naïve, she'd gotten mixed up with Johnny, then learned he was a wise guy, a "made man," cunning and vicious. Careful in her escape from him, she'd been sure there was time to come to the house, gather her belongings and get a good night's sleep before he realized she'd left him.

Wrong. Her hands tingled and her heart thundered in her ears. With a deep breath, she fought against her growing panic.

If the men didn't find what they wanted, she'd be dead soon. *Play for time.* "Tell me what you're looking for. Maybe I can find it for you."

"No more games. Give it up and I won't kill you."

He relaxed his hold for a second. She broke free and ran from the room.

Just as she reached for the front doorknob, the intruder caught her.

"Bitch!"

He pulled her into the living room as the smaller man dismantled the room. Down stuffing from the couch flew in the air as he slit open the pillows.

The man holding her pressed his hard body against hers. Then he rubbed her cheek with the back of his hand and ran his fingers through her hair.

"Blonde silk." He grinned for the first time.

She swallowed bile as a chill ran down her back.

"Bad things happen to little girls who steal," he whispered in her ear.

With one swift movement, he covered her lips with his. The odor of his pungent cologne sent nausea swirling in her. Hot breath and coarse stubble scraped against her face.

She bit him. He slapped her. She almost lost her balance and leaned against a wall for support.

A drop of blood formed on his split lip.

"This has been fun, Kelly, but you have to give it up." He held her chin and turned her face toward him. "Listen, bitch. I'm not leaving until I get it. If you're alive when I leave or you're dead, I don't care. Make it easy on yourself."

Kelly kicked him and sprinted for the front door, yelling all the way. She had the front door open when he grabbed her.

Just then, sirens blared; the noise drowned out her screams.

"Someone called the cops." The smaller guy sprinted out of the front door.

"I'll be back. You can run, but you can't hide from me." The attacker raised his hand. "Next time I get what I want or I'll kill you and I'll kill your sister too."

4

Shattered Rules

He shoved her from him with such force she flew back and hit the foyer wall. With a moan, she crumpled to the floor, the sound ceased and light became dark.

***

Brick Larson battled to keep his eyes open. After drinking three cups of coffee, acid burned his stomach. Still, there wasn't enough caffeine to keep him alert. Exhausted from a long work week, he'd planned to stay in Los Angeles to sleep away the weekend. But a churning in his gut sent him out into the night with a need to return home so powerful he could no longer deny the place he hadn't seen in five years.

He pushed down bitter memories. They didn't matter anymore. He hadn't meant to return. The FBI had transferred him back to San Francisco. However, he wasn't concerned. He'd moved on with his life.

He rubbed his eyes. *Focus on the road.* Highway 101 would have been an enjoyable ride. There were more places to stop and take a breather. Highway Five was just a long ribbon of boredom that stretched from one end of California to the other. But it was the fastest way home. Without driving greater than ten miles over the speed limit, he'd be in the Bay Area in six hours. The dashboard light caught his eye, ninety miles per hour. He let his foot off the gas pedal.

With his left hand on the steering wheel, he used his other one to rub his right knee. It throbbed from sitting in the same position for so long. His old injuries had healed, but sometimes late at night, he ached.

A car's horn blared. He swerved the wheel and brought the BMW M5 back into its lane. At the next gas station, he'd stop and buy another cup of coffee. By three thirty in the morning, he'd be home.

***

Fear woke Kelly with a jerk. She covered her mouth to stifle a scream. The intruders might still be in the house. Anxiety danced along her spine while she listened for sounds that the men were there—nothing.

The sirens from the nearby fire station must have frightened off the intruders. Living so close to the station, she'd often cursed the blaring noise that woke her late at night. Now she thanked God for it.

A dog barked and a car's engine sputtered. She looked up to see the front door standing wide open. She should close it. Too dizzy, she waited, not daring to move again.

Finally, she sat up. Her first instinct was to call the police. *I'll kill you and I'll kill your sister too.* The intruder's words rang in her ears. She couldn't phone officials until Carrie was safe.

The smartphone sat in the middle of the oak floor of the living room. She grabbed it and dialed her sister.

"Leave your name, number, and the date and time you called. I'll get back to you," Carrie's voicemail said.

*Shit. S*he'd always been able to reach her sister by phone—not today. *Dear God, p*lease let her be okay*.*

"Carrie, whatever you do, don't come home. Meet me at the Lake Tahoe cabin. Sorry, but I'm in trouble again. I'll explain when I see you." With a shaking hand, she disconnected the call and texted the same message.

A dull pain pulsed above her eyes. She rubbed her brow. What would her sister think when she heard the message? Ever since the death of their parents five years earlier, she and Carrie had had a rocky relationship. They'd shared their parent's house out of necessity due to the high cost of living in the San Francisco Bay Area. But they lived separate lives and rarely spoke to each other about anything but the running of their home.

Shattered Rules

Now, because of her stupidity in getting involved with Johnny Vega, her sister's life was in danger. She could blame FBI agent Ted Simmons if she wanted to play the "blame game." He was the one who talked her into taking Johnny's flash drive.

Once she'd learned the truth about her boyfriend and his involvement with the crime scene, she'd decided to end their relationship. It was then she met Agent Ted Simmons. He seemed such a nice, unassuming man and he needed her help.

"Do me a little favor," Agent Simmons had said. "It'll be easy. No big deal." He'd smiled at her.

She hadn't even asked what was on the flash drive. How could she turn him down? The FBI needed her. When Agent Simmons told her national security was involved, that had been enough. For the first time in a long time, she'd felt important, useful, and needed. Simmons had promised taking it would be simple. Nothing in her life had ever been straightforward. She should have remembered that. Too late now. She groaned. *You're an idiot.*

Still sitting on the floor, she looked up. Everything in the room was out of focus. She cradled her head between her knees and reached up to touch the lump on the back of her head. Could she drive with her sight so blurry? If not, how would she get away?

The neighbor's dog barked again.

A man stood in the front doorway, silhouetted by the driveway's light. Tense, she fisted her hands ready to fight if the intruder had returned. She squinted, hoping to see him better.

He entered.

"My God, what happened?"

"Brick." Though she hadn't heard it in five years, she knew his deep voice.

"Carrie?"

"No. I'm Kelly."

"You've grown up." He stared at her and then scanned the room. "What the hell happened?"

"Two men broke in and ransacked the house." She pushed her hair from her eyes and blinked several times to bring him into focus. His short blonde hair glistened in the room's light. Telltale lines of maturity lightly etched the corners of his full mouth.

"Are you okay?" He moved closer.

"I think so."

With the swift movement of an athlete, he came to her. "Can you stand?" His vivid teal eyes narrowed as he checked her out. "Need help?" Without waiting for an answer, he reached for her. His large hands steadied her until she found her balance.

She'd forgotten he was so tall, head and shoulders above her five feet four-inch height. She stared up into the face of the man she had secretly loved since she was a teenager.

"Is Carrie here too?"

"She's on a business trip." Kelly hesitated. "What are *you* doing here?"

"Tell me about it." He pointed to the living room.

A gnawing little voice in the back of her mind reminded her that Brick worked for the FBI. Yeah, he'd been engaged to her sister, but he *was* an agent. After not seeing him for years, what was he doing on her doorstep now? Why did he drive by the house in the middle of the night, tonight of all nights? Was it to see Carrie? Was he still in love with her sister, or could he be involved with the men who just ransacked the house?

8

The memory of Ted Simmons' words, roared in her ears, "The FBI has been infiltrated. Don't trust anyone except me."

Chilled, she pulled away from Brick.

Almost as if he understood her thoughts, his eyes narrowed. "I was driving back from LA. The nights are cooler. On a whim, I drove by the house and saw your front was open." He paused. "Have you called the police yet?"

"The intruders threatened to kill Carrie if I did."

A stunned expression spread across his handsome face. "The hell. How's she involved in this?"

"She's not." Kelly moaned.

"Are you hurt?"

"I bumped my head." She forced her lips into what she hoped was a reassuring smile. "It's nothing."

"Let me see." He reached for her and ran his hand over the back of her head.

She jumped back and ignored the desire to let him hold her. "I'm fine."

"That's quite a lump."

"I'm okay." She shivered under his scrutiny. "I am."

"Then let's get out of here."

"I can't. Carrie might come home. I called her cell, but she didn't answer. That's not like her. I'm worried. I sent a text, but I can't be sure she'll get it. I don't want her to come home and find the house like this." She waved her hand toward the ransacked living room.

"When are you expecting her?"

"Not for a couple of days, but what if she comes home early?"

"It's not safe to stay, Kelly. Those men could be back. You've got to get out."

She swallowed hard and glanced up to see his serious expression. "All right. Give me a minute."

In the bathroom, her body ached and her mind cried out for sleep. Even so, she splashed cold water on her face. *Think. What are you going to do?* She had to get away from Brick, retrieve the flash drive she'd hidden at Lake Tahoe and give it to Agent Simmons. Then everything would be okay. Her hands trembled as she rubbed her temples to stop the migraine that pulsed behind her eyes. Could she focus well enough to drive?

In her bedroom, she grabbed clean clothes off the floor and tossed them all into an overnight bag. She slipped on underpants and a bra and pulled on a pair of jeans and a white T-shirt. She found a black flat and hopped on one foot until she found the mate.

Relief flooded her when she found her wallet. The small amount of money she'd had was gone. At least it still held her driver's license.

Back in the entryway, Brick put a blue blazer over her shoulders. "I found it in the hall closet."

"Thanks." She stuffed the wallet in her jacket pocket.

"Let's get you someplace safe, then we can decide what to do next." He looked out of the living room window. "All clear."

"Fasten your seat belt," he said as the BMW sped away from the only home she had ever known.

When would it be safe to come home? Where was Brick taking her? She leaned back in the passenger seat and closed her eyes. It didn't matter as long as it was away from the house before the intruders returned.

If only she could tell Brick what was really going on, but Agent Simmons had said to trust no one.

Chapter 2

Brick had vowed it'd be a cold day in hell before he saw Carrie or Kelly Shaw again. Now, with Kelly sitting beside him, hurt and in danger, he didn't know what he wanted. He cursed his boss, Don McCallum, for asking him to take this undercover assignment.

At a stop sign, he glanced at Kelly. She purred in her sleep. He'd forgotten how small she was, delicate, but not fragile. There was a time when she was just his fiancée's playful kid sister. Back then, he'd barely noticed her. However, she'd grown. A dazzling female slept in the seat next to him. He noted the curve of her lips and the fullness of her breasts. Even hurt and exhausted, she oozed sex appeal. She wasn't the awkward teen he remembered.

He focused on the road and brought his mind back to the problem at hand. It was important to get the facts of what happened last night before time dulled her memory.

Years working at the FBI had taught him that sometimes it paid to be patient. She'd experienced trauma and needed rest. He'd find somewhere for them to stay. After a nap, he'd ask her to tell him, in detail, everything that happened last night.

The El Camino Motel in Redwood City was one of the few "mom and pop" motels left in the San Francisco Bay Area. The single-story adobe building with a red tiled roof was a middle-class haven, clean and relatively inexpensive. It was unlikely anyone would look for them there. He drove into the lot and parked, then glanced at her again. *Too damned sexy.*

"Kelly, wait in the car while I register."

On the way to the motel's office, he passed the empty swimming pool. No one would see him go into the lobby.

When they entered the motel room, he took a deep breath. Fresh air, no musty smells like many of the rooms he'd stayed in during his other undercover assignments. Though the inn was built in a California adobe style, the rooms were themed. The bamboo furniture, upholstered in pink, green, and gray floral fabric, had to be someone's misguided idea of Hawaiian décor. A framed picture of Mount Kilauea hung over the queen-size bed. He smiled at the choice of Hawaiian decorations in the Spanish-style motel.

"There's only one bed."

"Kelly, we're lucky they had a room." He pulled one of the pillows and the bedspread off the bed and threw them onto the maroon wall-to-wall carpeting. "I'll bunk on the floor."

"No. I can't let you do that. I shouldn't even be here. I should be driving to Lake Tahoe, but I can't seem to keep my eyes focused. Still, I'm not going to take your bed."

"I got it for you."

"If I could only get rid of this headache." She sat on the bed, lay back, and closed her eyes.

Did she have a concussion? She seemed alert. Not since his days as an army medic in South Korea had he checked for dilated pupils. Nonetheless, in twenty

12

minutes, he'd examine her. He set his smartphone's alarm. If her condition worsened, he'd take her to a hospital emergency room.

He breathed in her feminine scent, then shook off the need to touch her. He shouldn't be in a motel room with his ex-fiancé's sexy little sister. He'd have said no to this assignment if anyone but his boss, Don McCallum, had asked. Years earlier, when he was badly injured in an ambush, his boss had helped him and stuck by him when others suggested he should take disability and early retirement. He owed Don.

The FBI was looking for information on a thug named Johnny Vega, a gangster connected to organized crime, involved in illegal gambling, money laundering, and now possible espionage.

While attending the University of Nevada's Reno campus, Kelly had become Johnny Vega's girlfriend. She looked so innocent. Brick reminded himself she wasn't as sweet as she appeared, or she wouldn't be Johnny's girl.

Brick's boss hoped to get a lead on Vega's activities through Kelly. Because of Brick's history with Kelly's sister, he was the FBI's first choice for this assignment.

It was supposed to be straightforward, stop by the house and explain that he was back in the area. Chat with Carrie and Kelly, then direct the conversation to Johnny Vega. He'd get whatever information he could and leave. He didn't understand what made him drive by the house in the middle of the night. Thank God he had. With Kelly in danger, things weren't so clear-cut anymore.

The soft purring of Kelly's breathing filled the room as she slept. Her blazer and jeans hung on the back of a chair and her perfectly shaped, bikini-clad, backside peeked out from under the white sheets.

His blood heated and his body tightened. Restless, he paced the room and then looked out of the window to the parking lot. He didn't think anyone knew his car, but it couldn't hurt to play it safe. He'd move the BMW away from their motel room door.

He drove to the other side of the lot and parked behind a massive heritage oak tree. As he walked back to the room, he rotated his neck to release the tension in his tightly flexed muscles.

Still asleep, she hadn't moved since he left the room. He pulled the blackout drapes closed and stretched out on the maroon carpet. With the pillow fluffed, he pulled the flowered bedspread around him. After the long drive from LA, exhaustion gnawed at him. Still, thinking about sleeping in the same room as Kelly only increased his tension.

His knee ached, no surprise there. It always did when he didn't get enough sleep, something that was happening too often these days.

The enticing aroma of Kelly's perfume floated in the air. He ignored the fragrance and forced his eyes closed. A vision of her in the bed, with her rear peeking out from the sheets, sent a pang of lust to poke him. *Keep your mind on the job. Get the information on Johnny Vega and get the hell out.*

***

The intruder turned off the engine and leaned back in the cab of a rented pick-up truck. He twisted the signet ring on his index finger and smiled. He could just see the fender of the M5 parked behind a tree in the parking lot of the El Camino Motel. If he hadn't seen the car pull into the space, he would have missed it.

"Let the girl go and follow her," his boss had said. "When she feels safe, she'll get what we want."

Shattered Rules

It was just a matter of time until she retrieved the flash drive. He grinned because he'd be there when she did.

The fear he'd seen in the girl's eyes sent a sense of power rushing through him. He recalled the feel of her and his breathing quickened. In a little while, he'd have her trembling against him again. When he did, he'd make her beg to give him anything he wanted. Once he got the flash drive, he could have her. He'd take everything she could give and then make sure her body was never found.

A nine-millimeter pistol lay on the seat next to him. He reached for the cold steel. It felt good in his hand. The guy protecting the girl looked like he could take care of himself. It didn't matter. He might be a hard ass, but he couldn't outrun a bullet.

***

The alarm went off in the darkened motel room. Brick forced his eyes open and stretched. Expected pain flared in his right knee. He rubbed it, then limped the short distance to the bed and felt for the bedside lamp.

"Brick?" Kelly raised her hand to cover her eyes from the glare of the light.

"Yeah."

"What's wrong?"

"Nothing. I'm going to check your pupils, see if you're okay. It'll only take a minute."

"I'm fine."

"Yeah. I know, but you've got a lump on the back of your head."

With a penlight he had on his key chain, he checked her pupils' reaction to light. "Eyes look fine."

"Can I go back to sleep?"

"Humor me and answer a couple of questions."

"Okay."

"What day is it?"

"Saturday." She sat up and adjusted her T-shirt.

He pretended not to notice the curve of her breasts and the tightness of her nipples pressing against the cotton fabric.

She glanced up at him and pulled the white sheet to her chin.

He cleared his throat and forced his gaze to meet hers. "What month is it?"

"June." She yawned.

She seemed awfully tired. A symptom of head trauma, but considering what she went through last night, exhaustion was to be expected. She roused easily enough and her pupils were equal and reactive. But to be on the safe side, he decided to continue checking on her every hour.

"Can I sleep now?"

"Go ahead," he said more gruffly than he meant to.

She frowned, touched the back of her head, and moaned.

Anger towards the intruders surged in him. Guilt for not telling her the reason for coming to see her gnawed at him.

She lay down and pulled up all the covers.

He set the alarm again, then turned off the light.

In his makeshift bed on the floor, he stared into the darkness.

An hour later, his alarm went off. Cold and stiff, he rolled to a sitting position.

"Don't even think about getting up. I know what month it is, where I am, and the name of the president of the United States. If you turn on a light and try to jab me in the eye, I'll scream."

"Okay." He laughed. "Go back to sleep." This was the spunky female he remembered. She might be sore from her bruises, but she was going to be all right. Finally, able to admit his exhaustion, he lay back and let sleep overtake him.

Light peeked into the room through a slit where the two gaudy pink drapes didn't completely meet. He had no idea how long he'd been sleeping. He checked his cell. It was five in the morning. His stomach growled. He'd noticed a twenty-four-hour supermarket nearby. He could run out and buy a few things, and return before Kelly woke up.

The door closed silently behind him.

***

The intruder gulped the last drop of the putrid coffee he'd bought from a nearby diner. He spit out some grounds and wiped his mouth. Kelly's protector had just left the motel room. She was alone. He smiled.

Out of the pick-up truck, he jogged to the back of the motel. Through the partially open drapes, he peered into a room. The outline of the girl sleeping in a T-shirt and panties, the bedding bundled at her feet, could be seen in the early light. "Gotcha."

He could grab her right now. Motel door locks couldn't stop him. While he thought about it, he leaned closer to the window and stared through the slit in the drapes again. *Sexy bitch.*

***

Kelly moaned. The intruder's hands were on her again, touching her, and pulling her close. His cigarette breath made her stomach lurch. She tried to run. He held her. Pain ran down her arm. Then he kissed her. "No!" she screamed, jerked to a sitting position in bed, and opened her eyes. With her hand on her heart, she fought to breathe.

17

For a moment she didn't know where she was. Slowly, the memory of Brick taking her to the motel returned. The pillow and blanket he'd used were still on the floor. He was nowhere in sight.

She jumped out of bed. "Are you in there?" She knocked on the bathroom door and it creaked open. *Empty. Abandoned.* He'd left without a word.

Panic sent a tremor through her.

She glanced back into the motel room. A man stared through the fissure in the drapes. A second later, the motel door clicked open.

She searched the room for a weapon.

Brick walked into the room carrying a grocery bag and a cardboard tray with two huge cups of coffee.

Still dressed in her T-shirt and panties, Kelly stood in the middle of the room. The bedside lamp she'd ripped from the wall plug was held high as if it were a weapon. The electrical cord dangled to the floor.

"What the hell, Kelly? You planning to hit me?"

"Brick, someone was watching me through the window. I thought he was coming into the room to get me."

His smile vanished. Before she could say more, he dropped the grocery bag and set the cups of coffee on the floor. "Stay in the room, away from the window," he shouted as he ran out the door.

She started to run after him, then remembered she was only wearing her underwear.

She slammed the door and locked it.

Her hands trembled as she pulled on her jeans and T-shirt. She couldn't stay in the room. What if Brick needed her? He could be hurt by the intruder. Without thinking how angry he might be if she left the room, she rushed out the door.

Chapter 3

Kelly came around the corner of the motel and bumped into Brick.

"I see you can't follow directions. Kelly, you were supposed to stay inside."

Before she could answer, he said, "Doesn't matter now. The asshole got away. Probably some pervert who hangs around motels. The jerk hopped the back fence and disappeared." He took a deep breath. "You okay?"

"A little scared."

Back in the room, she picked up the grocery bag and the paper cups. "Coffee smells good," she said to change the conversation, feeling foolish because she'd assumed the intruder had found her.

She set everything on the table.

Brick yanked strawberry yogurt, blueberry muffins and navel oranges from the bag.

Under ordinary circumstances, she'd have welcomed the yogurt. Today, her stomach recoiled at the thought of eating. Even if she wanted something, she doubted she could force food down her tightened throat.

She should be driving to Lake Tahoe to get and deliver the flash drive to Agent Simmons. She'd wanted to mail it to him. Simmons felt it wasn't safe because someone else could open the package. It had to be put into his hands in person.

Brick opened the drapes and sat down at the table. Kelly joined him and watched as he downed two muffins and a container of yogurt. His appetite obviously hadn't been affected by what happened today. He peeled an orange and the aroma of citrus filled the room.

Content to keep the conversation at bay, she sipped her coffee and stared out of the window. The morning breeze made white caps on the surface of the water in the swimming pool. The wind mingled with the fog from the hills. In her own fog, she wished the mist would lift and show her if she could trust Brick.

In a while, she'd have to answer questions about what happened last night—honest answers. Stress increased the acid in her stomach. Could she respond well enough to satisfy him without bringing up the flash drive or Agent Simmons? Brick had to be convinced to let her go without talking to the authorities.

She glanced at him as he leaned back in the chair. His lean body appeared taut and more muscled than it had years earlier. A tough veneer had aged his incredibly handsome features.

"Feeling better?" He reached for her hand and gently squeezed it.

"Yeah." She could have told him his touch caused a fire to course through her, and she felt an emotion she didn't want to define.

He seemed content to continue holding her hand. However, she pulled away to stop the fever he'd started in her. She held the paper cup with both hands. The hot coffee was cool in comparison to his touch.

Silence filled the room.

He cleared his throat. "Tell me what happened last night."

She fidgeted with the plastic lid on the cup.

As he watched her, she could feel his annoyance, then noticed impatience tighten his full lips into a thin line.

She walked to the window. Here in Redwood City, the sun fought to break through the dense mist. Could she tell Brick what was really going on? She wanted to, but living with Johnny Vega had taught her to mistrust people. What if Brick was working with Johnny? Maybe he was here to watch her and report back to her ex-boyfriend. Improbable as that might seem, her life and Carrie's depended on making the right decision.

"Kelly, the last time I saw you, you were just a kid. What did you do after high school?"

"What?" The question was so unexpected, that for a minute, she didn't answer.

"After high school?" He prompted and leaned back in the chair with his long legs stretched out in front of him as if he had nothing else to do but enjoy a leisurely conversation.

He was using small talk to put her at ease. It only increased her tension and made her even more wary of him.

"Kelly."

"I went to the University of Nevada. With the casinos and all, I thought Reno would be exciting. I was wrong." She hesitated. "I've gotten an education all right. I've learned how easy it is to be duped by people who tell you they love you." She heard the bitterness in her voice but couldn't stop it. "I've learned how easy it is to be hurt by people you believed you could trust. I've learned how easy it is to lose control of my life. I've learned how—oh never mind." She turned away in time to wipe a tear before he saw it.

She glanced back at him. "Don't pay any attention to me. I'm upset. None of this is your problem." She paused as pain throbbed in her right temple. "Did you happen to buy aspirin? I've got a killer headache."

He pulled a bottle out of the paper bag. "There's a hairbrush, a toothbrush, toothpaste, and deodorant in there too."

"Thanks." She gulped down two tablets with her coffee.

"I have to take a shower. I want to wash away the touch of those men." She hesitated. "I didn't mean to say that out loud."

He fisted his right hand. "Do you need a doctor? Did they rape you?"

"No. Uh, I'm okay." She pushed down the memory of tasting the stranger's blood after she bit him.

Brick frowned and looked down, preventing her from reading the exposed reaction in his eyes.

"Thanks for helping me yesterday." He was so near she could touch him but thought better of it.

Their eyes caught. Raw emotion flamed in his expression.

With the items he'd bought for her, she ran into the bathroom.

In the shower stall, she let the hot water pound her stressed muscles and cursed herself for getting involved with Johnny Vega. Even though she'd been warned by friends that he was mob-connected and to stay away from him, she'd let his charming smile entice her. At that time, the Mob meant nothing to her. It was a figment of Hollywood's imagination. A TV show to entertain the masses.

Shattered Rules

Johnny wanted her. After the accidental death of her parents, she needed someone to care for her. At first, he'd been kind and tender. He made her feel beautiful. She'd been vulnerable. It was easy to understand that today. Back then, she'd believed he loved her. Now, she laughed at her stupidity.

The concern Johnny had shown her in public was just a veneer. In private, she found a cruel, sadistic man, and discovered what terror felt like. Love and hate were two sides of the same emotion, and he showed her both. Quickly, the dire consequences of crossing him became known to her.

Even under the flow of hot water, she shivered. *You're free of him now. Don't think about Johnny.*

She turned off the spray, towel dried, and brushed her hair with the new brush Brick had given her. Her hair was just long enough to hide most of the purple bruising on her shoulder caused by the intruder.

Dressed in a white tank top and blue jeans, she stepped into the dark leather flats.

"The bathroom's all yours," she said as she entered the bedroom.

***

The masculine scent of shaving cream wafted into the room when Brick opened the bathroom door and returned to the bedroom. Water glistened in his short blonde hair and his facial stubble was gone.

Her gaze traveled from his navy runners to his blue jeans. She tracked long muscular legs, then followed them to the tapered waist that led to his muscled torso. His broad shoulders were draped in a navy polo shirt.

*Whoa. S*he took a breath.

"I'd like to talk about what happened yesterday." He sat down at the table again. "Maybe you'll remember something that'll help us figure out who those men are."

"I don't like to think about it." She hesitated. "Don't know if I *can* talk about it."

"You have to." He tensed and his right hand flexed.

Pain pulsed in her temples. Maybe if she told him part of the truth, he'd let her leave. "What do you want to know?"

"Just start from the beginning. What happened when the intruders entered the house? Let the events play like a movie in your head. Concentrate on the things that can't be changed like the color of skin, height, and bone structure."

"Uh, let me think." She rubbed her temples. "The first guy was in his early thirties, about your height, with dark eyes."

"Okay, about six feet three inches. What else?"

"Muscular build, high cheekbones, and a straight nose." She paused and strained to recall the guy.

"He's big-boned, has dark wavy hair, and an olive complexion. And he enjoys causing pain." She tried but couldn't stop her voice from shaking. "I saw it in his eyes when he hit me."

Brick flinched. "Anything else?"

She forced her mind back to the moment the man grabbed her. "Uh, he wore a signet ring. I didn't remember that until now. It had a gold band and a black stone and with the gold initial "N" in the center of the stone." She rubbed her sore arm and remembered seeing the ring when he grabbed her.

"I thought he was a delivery man or I'd never have opened the door. I told you Carrie is on a business trip.

The airline lost one of her suitcases. I thought he was returning it."

"The guy wasn't worried about his ring being recognized. Maybe he wanted you to know who he was or he is not from around here and knew you wouldn't recognize it."

"I'd never seen him or it before."

"And the second guy?"

She took a deep breath before answering. "He was in his late twenties, on the short side of average. I'm not too good at guessing height, but I don't think he was more than five feet eight. Thin. I really didn't see his eyes for more than a second, brown, I think. I know his hair was straight and dark. He spoke with an East Coast accent, maybe a borough in New York City?"

"Good. You're doing great. Did they call each other by name?"

"No."

Brick kept the questions coming and she did her best to answer them.

"A brown van was parked in front of the house. The driveway light illuminated it. It looked just like the delivery vans you see all over the city."

"Could have been. Maybe they stole it. Did you see the license plate?"

She squeezed her eyes closed and let the event play in her mind. "Uh, L, M." She stopped. "Three, one, six, I think. That's all I can remember."

"That's not a commercial license plate." He noted it in his cell phone. "That plate should be on a car. I'll make some discreet inquiries. Your name won't be mentioned."

"Thanks."

"Whoever the intruders were, they knew you'd be home."

"You're scaring me."

"You should be afraid." He frowned. "It'd be easier if you went to an FBI office. The men might be on file and you could identify them."

"No FBI. Don't you understand, the man said he'd kill Carrie if I talked to the authorities? I know you're right about it being easier to identify them. What if the intruders found out? I can't take a chance with my sister's life."

She paced the room and then said, "Please let me talk to Carrie. Let her know she's in danger." The headache was back, pounding over her right eye.

He stared at her but didn't answer.

Again, she resisted the urge to touch him. Instead, she moved away. He wasn't going to agree. He wanted the authorities involved.

He stepped closer to her and bent down, so near she thought he might kiss her. With lips parted in anticipation, she waited.

He grunted and walked to the window and glanced out. "I don't want you or Carrie to get hurt."

Astonished by her feelings of disappointment, she stood transfixed. He wanted to kiss her. She saw it in his eyes. He didn't. Why?

"The ransacking of your home is a matter for the local police. Eventually, you're going to have to talk to them," he said his voice stern.

"I'll—I just need to see Carrie first."

"Don't wait too long."

"I won't. I promise."

"We better get going."

We? Was he planning to stay with her until she talked to Carrie? She couldn't allow that. "Take me home to get my car. I'm going to drive to the cabin." She shook her head to make sure the room was still in focus and she could drive.

"It's over a four-hour drive to Lake Tahoe. After what's happened to you, it's not a good idea to go alone. There are too many places you could be waylaid."

"I'll be fine. I've driven to the cabin many times."

"Damn, Kelly. It's different this time. Don't you realize the trouble you're in? Grow up."

"Damn, Brick," she mimicked his tone of voice. "I owe it to my sister to talk to her without the police or FBI, she said pointedly. "I can't get her on her cell, but Carrie is coming to the cabin. Don't you understand? Give me a chance to speak to her." Her back muscles tensed as her voice rose.

"Hey, I care about Carrie too."

"Do you? I'm surprised. After the way she broke off the engagement, I'd think you'd hate her."

He winced. "What happened between your sister and me was a long time ago. It's not important anymore."

He said it didn't matter, but she saw his expression harden as he talked about Carrie.

"I'm going home to get my car with or without your help. You can't keep me here."

"Don't push me, Kelly, or you'll find out what I can do." He glared at her.

"Would you arrest me when I only want to warn my sister?"

Silence filled the room.

"Okay," he said.

"Okay, what?"

"I'll take you to get your car if you're sure that's what you want. But if you run into trouble on the way to the lake, you'll be on your own. I won't be there to save your ass."

Chapter 4

Princeton Street, lined by two and three-bedroom cottages with manicured gardens, appeared quiet. A neighbor washed an SUV in his driveway and a couple of young boys walked toward the park. It looked like any US residential street on a Saturday. No one would guess Kelly's life had been threatened and her house ransacked on this idyllic lane.

The small single-story white stucco house, with beige shutters and a terracotta stone driveway, looked normal. Daisies smiled a welcome from a green ceramic pot on the front porch and a small silver wind chime tinkled hello. Instead of her usual feeling of comfort, her heart pounded and her breathing became ragged.

Brick drove slowly by her house and continued around the block. "See anything unusual, something out of place in the neighborhood?"

"Everything looks fine."

He continued around the block and parked in front of her home. "Stay here while I check out the house."

"The keys to my car are hanging on the hook in the entry hall closet," she said.

"Okay."

Impatient, while she waited for him, she drummed her fingers on the armrest. What was taking him so long? A car backfired and she jumped as fear slashed her. She scanned the neighborhood. The guy across the street continued to wash his car and didn't bother to glance in the direction of the noise.

She sighed. Maybe when she got to the cabin at the lake, she'd feel safe again.

Brick came out of the garage and walked toward her.

He opened the car door. "Walk in front of me, straight into the garage. I'll be right behind you."

He shielded her. She didn't see his gun, but his body language told her he had one.

Did he think someone was watching the house? She walked quickly up the driveway.

As her eyes adjusted to the dim light in the garage, she noticed the shelves were empty. The contents lay strewn on the floor.

Damn the intruders. Damn, Johnny. Damn my stupidity for getting involved with him.

"Kelly, your car's fine. I checked."

"Thank God." She got into the driver's seat. "I had it tuned up last week and filled the gas tank."

He put her bag in the trunk and then went around to the driver's side of the car.

"Here's my card. If you need anything, call me anytime, day or night."

Her hand brushed his as she took it. She pulled back as if touching hot metal. If he noticed, he didn't say anything.

"Kell, I mean call day or night."

What could she say to him? Thank you seemed inadequate. Confused feelings tore at her. Half of her wanted to stay with him and half of her wanted to get away as soon as possible.

This might be the last time she'd see Brick. He'd go back to his current life, whatever that was, and never be heard from again. All she'd have was a memory of a girlhood crush and a debt she could never repay.

"I should go with you, Kelly." He paused. "Watch yourself."

"I will." She drove out of the garage and down the driveway. Before turning left, she looked in the rear mirror. Brick stood in the driveway watching her, the garage door closing behind him, his expression stern.

***

The intruder noticed the girl driving by his parked truck. Kelly didn't see him, didn't turn her head in his direction, but fear gripped her features. He drove the pick-up truck from the curb and followed her car, careful not to get too close to the old Honda.

He remembered the kiss he'd stolen and ran his finger over the cut on his lip. She owed him. His body tightened. He'd make her pay. The boss promised him a bonus when he delivered the flash drive. The only thing he wanted was the girl.

***

Brick watched Kelly's car disappear down the street. She meant nothing to him, just an insignificant person from his past. Yet watching her drive out of his life, a feeling of loss washed over him.

He remembered her slumped on the entryway floor. "Hell!" When he first saw her, he thought she was dead. Later, bruised and confused, she lay on the bed in the motel helpless and more fragile than he'd ever seen her. A sudden need to protect her spiked in him.

A pragmatist, he spent his days working with facts and figures, right and wrong. He didn't get personally involved in his cases, but she was personal and too damned close to the past he wanted to forget.

Shit. He should have demanded that he drive her to Tahoe. Still, if the intruders were watching the house, she'd be in danger if she were seen driving off with a known FBI agent. She must be seen going alone.

He reassured himself that if the intruders had wanted her dead, yesterday he would have found her lifeless body.

The people threatening her were casting her out with enough line to give her a sense of freedom, so, she'd get what they wanted. When she had it, they'd reel her in. He wished he knew just where and when that would happen.

During his engagement to Kelly's sister, he'd spent a weekend at the Shaw's Tahoe cabin. He'd be there before Kelly arrived.

In the driver's seat of his vehicle, he pulled out his cell and punched in his boss's number.

On a Saturday morning, Don would be at home with his wife and two kids. The man often complained about the hardship of raising a family on an FBI salary, especially in the San Francisco Bay Area where the cost of living was one of the highest in the nation. However, he always complained with a smile. Don doted on his wife and kids. A twinge of envy pricked Brick.

His boss answered the phone on the second ring.

"I made contact." He gave him a quick rundown of recent events, including the descriptions of the intruders and the license plate of the van seen in her driveway. "Send a team to her house and bag and tag anything you find. You've got the address on Princeton Street, Palo Alto, right?"

"Yeah, I got it and your wish is my command." Don laughed and then became serious. "Something's up. I got a memo saying the Bureau opened a PI file on Kelly."

"Why? I thought Johnny Vega was the person of interest."

"Guess somebody thinks she may be involved in his deals, not just in his bed."

The thought of Johnny Vega touching Kelly sent anger charging through him. It was disgusting enough she was Johnny's girlfriend. Could she be involved with his shady deals as well? If she were, it would break Carrie's heart.

"Look, the sooner you find out what Vega is up to, the sooner we can make some sense out of all this," Don continued. "And be careful. The people after her are playing for keeps." He paused. "Did you hear Jack Anson, one of our agents working undercover on this case, is dead? His bullet-riddled body was found floating face down in the Truckee River this morning."

"Shit."

"The Reno police are keeping it under wraps. They are calling it a drowning." Don cleared his throat. "He was in somebody's way. Watch yourself."

"I hear you."

"Online chatter says something big is going down. Reno is the epicenter and Johnny Vega's name keeps coming up. Kelly is our only way of getting information on him. I need you to stay with it. Do whatever you have to and get her back in your sights. Don't let her out of it again. She knows something. I want to understand what."

"Okay."

"And buddy, I've seen her photo. She's a tasty piece of ass. Lay a hand on a gangster's bitch and you can kiss your FBI career goodbye."

Shattered Rules

Brick gripped the phone so hard he thought it might crack, but he didn't respond.

"I didn't tell you, Brick, but after you were ambushed and, in the hospital, the brass wanted you riding a desk," Don continued. "I went to bat for you then. So, don't let me down."

"I won't." He relaxed his grip. Don had no right to call Kelly names. Still, his boss was correct about one thing; if he got involved with her, he *could* kiss his FBI career goodbye. She was sexy, but not so luscious that he'd let her destroy his career. Nothing and no one was going to prevent him from doing his job.

"And Brick, I don't want to get a memo telling me you've been found floating face down in Lake Tahoe."

"You and me both."

It was damned irritating that Don hadn't asked him to stay with Kelly earlier. Still, this made it easier for him because he'd never had any intention of letting her handle the situation alone. He wouldn't touch her, but he'd protect her.

He drove toward the Oakland Airport. An image of the dead agent flashed in his mind. Jack, a quiet man with a quick smile, was killed while checking into Johnny Vega's dealings. Brick would damn well watch his own back and he'd get Kelly's too.

He wondered if she understood the danger of her circumstances. She seemed to reject the truth, driving off alone. He'd seen too many crime victims live in denial until it was too late. As far as her taking part in Johnny's crimes, he didn't believe it. The young teenager he'd known wouldn't become involved in anything criminal. She was all grown up now. He sucked in the air. Was he living in denial too?

33

The intruders told Kelly they'd kill her and her sister. He stomped on the gas pedal and sped toward the local airport.

A chartered plane would get him to the Truckee, California airport. While he waited for the flight, he made arrangements to rent a Volvo from a small company that didn't mark their rental cars. A nondescript car would be waiting for him when he arrived.

***

The gray sedan took the mountain turns with ease. Away from the bustle of the San Francisco Bay Area, Brick breathed in the scent of fresh pine air. He smiled at the intense colors of the Sierra Nevada Mountains. The forest green of the Sugar and Ponderosa pine trees stood out against the deep blue sky. A damn shame he wasn't here to enjoy what the resort area had to offer.

In a mini-mart restroom, he donned black ski pants and a teal ski sweater. A down parka and a Mylar blanket waited in his pack.

It took less than thirty minutes to reach Tahoe City. Though he hadn't been to the Shaw Cabin in five years, he found it easily.

A small graveled road overlooking the cabin led to Lake Tahoe. Fishermen used it to launch their boats. From the graveled road he could keep an eye on the cabin without being seen. Sheltered by a grove of Ponderosa pines, he backed onto the road and faced the cabin.

The arts and crafts structure, with its redwood walls and weathered copper roof, jutted up through a grove of birch and pine, the lake just a few steps from its boundary. The last time he'd visited the cabin it had been in pristine condition. Now, the green trim around the windows had faded. The front steps, weathered by years of snow, looked as if they might give way. A cord of firewood lay beside the driveway waiting to be stacked. The place cried out for a man's attention.

The memory of making love with Carrie on the deck overlooking the lake flashed. He shook it away and pushed down the lost dream of a wife and kids. He got out of the car and walked toward the home.

At the cabin, he glanced through the cobweb-covered garage window. The interior was empty. At the front porch, he pulled on the wooden screen door. It squeaked open. The black wrought iron knocker on the front door made a hollow sound. He banged on it again and waited. No answer. He turned the front door handle—locked.

It took less than two minutes to find the extra house key hidden in a small metal box above the front door. Would people never learn?

"Hello, anyone home?" he shouted as he entered. "Anybody here?"

The interior looked as it had years earlier when he'd been engaged to Kelly's sister. *Home.* It wasn't his home. It never would be. A twinge of regret jabbed him. *Forget it. It doesn't matter now.*

He glanced at the aged wooden paneling and the plush forest green carpet. In the great room, the hearth of the huge river rock fireplace was cold. Undisturbed by human hands, a layer of dust covered the cotton fabric that draped the mission-style furniture.

He searched each room, careful not to leave a trace of having been there. There was no sign the rooms had been used recently.

He left the cabin, locked the front door, and dropped the extra house key into his pocket.

With his lengthy body stuffed into the Volvo's shorter space, he reclined the seat. Lack of sleep was beginning to take its toll and his muscles ached. He had a night standing guard ahead of him, better snatch some shut-eye before Kelly arrived. He set the alarm to ring in two hours and closed his eyes.

Later, he jerked awake, turned off the alarm and rubbed his stiff neck then looked toward Donner Pass. Black clouds had formed over the mountains where Kelly would drive. The wind whistled through the trees and the sky grew darker. However, if things went smoothly, she'd beat the gathering storm and be at the cabin before it started.

The temperature dropped and the sky threatened to snow. He pulled on his parka, revved the car's engine, and turned on the heater for a moment.

Snow began to fall. The cobblestone driveway turned from gray to white and still, Kelly didn't arrive.

A numbing cold invaded the car. He rubbed his hands together to bring back the feeling in his fingertips. He cursed himself for letting her go and strained to see through the increasing veil of flakes. As snow hit his face, he blinked to clear it away and searched the horizon. *Kelly, where the hell are you?*

Chapter 5

Kelly's ears pulsed from the pressure of the higher altitude. Still wearing only her white cotton tank top and jeans, she shivered. The clothes had been perfect for the heat of the Sacramento Valley, but not for the Sierra Nevada Mountains. If she'd thought about it, she'd have taken her sweater out of the trunk when she stopped at a gas station in Auburn.

A snowflake landed on the Honda's windshield, surprising weather for June. In a Sierra Nevada minute, the weather changed, much as her life had, from a sunny day to a blizzard.

Highway Eighty winding toward Donner Summit was nearly white. On high, the wipers struggled to slide across the windshield, barely able to move the heavy snow.

Against the wall of wind and ice, Kelly drove the vintage car up the grade toward the seven thousand-foot summit. The engine strained and the gauge on the dashboard edged dangerously close to the red zone, indicating the engine was overheating. She wiped the condensation from the front window.

The snow might have lulled her into watching its beauty if she weren't worried she was driving too close to the edge of the road that bordered the cliff. Jerking on the wheel, she steered the car toward the middle of the road. She gasped as an SUV coming from the opposite direction almost sideswiped her car.

Ghostlike headlights of a vehicle flashed in the rearview mirror. A classic black Cadillac closed in on her car. The driver must not be able to see her small white car. She tapped the brake pedal to flash the Honda's scarlet brake lights.

Like a leopard, the dark car lunged toward her, racing toward the bumper. She stomped on the gas pedal, but her car's tires spun in the snow. She screamed, expecting the Cadillac's impact.

At the last second, the driver slammed on the brakes. The vehicle went into a spin, hurling toward the Honda. A wall of snow and ice shot high into the air and landed on the Caddy, turning it white.

In the rear mirror, she watched in horror as the luxury car hit the embankment on the other side of the road. It came to a stop facing the wrong direction on the highway. Steam rose from the dying engine, but the Caddy's headlights were still bright. She left the engine running, pulled on the hand brake, and rushed out to check on the other driver. He might be hurt.

As she ran toward the wrecked car, the wind assaulted her, sending ice into her eyes and nose. She coughed and brushed it away. A gust of wind nearly knocked her over. Her leather flats had no traction on the snow and she slipped on the icy road. Still, she got up and pushed into the wind, moving toward the disabled vehicle.

When she reached it, the driver's side door flew open. An enormous man jumped out and grabbed her arm. She shrieked and twisted out of his grasp, fell, and scrambled to her feet, jogging out of his reach. He yelled at her. Most of his words were lost in the wind gusts. He yelled again, his voice a roaring noise of undecipherable words. The only one she understood, die.

She gasped. The cold air burned her lungs. She sprinted toward the Honda and glanced back. The man was running after her.

She increased her speed and almost lost her footing.

Damn, where's my car? She squinted to see through the snowstorm and searched for her white vehicle. Barely visible in the storm, the car's engine was still turning over. She leaped into the driver's seat and put the transmission in first. Her wet shoe slipped off the clutch and the car stalled. She turned the key, but the engine didn't start.

She looked behind her and saw the man coming closer. Dressed in black, his suit was now spotted with snow. The anger on his face was intense as he trudged in her direction. His right hand flexed around a tire iron.

In a second, he'd be at her car. She stomped on the clutch and turned the key again. "Start. Damn it. Start."

Just as the man grabbed the Honda's door handle, the car's engine turned over and the car pitched forward. The handle was yanked from the guy's grip and he fell to his knees in the snow.

Kelly snatched a quick look in the rear mirror as she drove away. The man struggled to his feet. His black clothes were now fully covered in snow. He shook his fist at her and his face went crimson.

When she couldn't see him anymore, she slowed the car, but couldn't slow her rapid heartbeat.

"Die." his threat echoed in her ears again. Was this road rage from a crazy man or did he have something to do with Johnny? She checked the mirror, no Cadillac, only darkness. She let her shoulders relax, but her heart rate refused to return to normal.

As the storm worsened, the highway disappeared under a blanket of white powder. Without landmarks, it was impossible to know where to drive.

Her hands ached from squeezing the steering wheel. If she stopped driving, the man chasing her would have time to start his Cadillac and catch up to her.

Tears froze on her cheeks. Reckless as it might be, her only option was to keep going and risk plunging off the seven-thousand-foot drop from Donner Summit.

***

The Shaw bungalow was dark and so were the neighboring houses. Hours had passed since anyone had come down the quiet street that led to Kelly Shaw's cabin.

The wind slammed against the Volvo and the snow blocked Brick's view of the mountains. If it was this bad here, he could only imagine how awful the storm was on Donner Summit.

He thought about clearing the flakes off the windshield, but the snow was coming down so fast it wasn't worth the effort. Standing outside his vehicle, he strained to see Highway Eighty.

In this weather, an accident could leave Kelly on the summit hurt and isolated. Futile tension tightened his chest.

Hell. It was his fault for letting her go.

***

With the road covered in snow, Kelly could only guess if it turned or continued straight ahead. She took her foot off the gas pedal and the car slowed. Maybe she'd die of hypothermia, but that was better than plunging off Donner Summit. Wasn't it?

The hood of her car was completely covered in snow now. Before long, it would disappear under the white

40

stuff. She strained to see out of the small space still clear on the windshield.

The wind shifted and suddenly in the sea of white, her eye caught a flash of red. There it was again. A semi-tractor/ trailer rig seemed to rise before her eyes. A red letter marked the eighteen-wheeler's back door, the logo of a familiar supermarket chain.

The truck's many tires melted the snow as it drove over the powder, leaving a narrow trail. She steered the Honda's tires into the tracks.

The big rig picked up speed.

Damn. Her breathing quickened as she increased the car's speed. She hoped the driver of the rig had a better view than she did. In the whiteout, she had no idea where the driver was going, but without the rig to follow, she was lost.

The truck reached the top of the summit and quickly sped down the grade. To keep up with it, she pressed down the gas pedal. Her grip on the wheel was so hard her fingers ached, but she held her car in the eighteen-wheeler's path.

A gust of wind hit her car. It shuddered; the windows shook as the auto picked up speed on the downhill. The rig's brake light flashed and she slammed both feet on the brakes as the Honda slid on the icy road toward the rig. She braced for impact. Just before she rear-ended the truck, the Honda came to a halt.

The double-wheeler moved again. She managed to keep her car close enough to see the rig, but not too near. Gradually, the downgrade became less steep. She loosened her grip on the steering wheel and took a slow deep breath.

They drove into the outskirts of the small resort town of Truckee, California. She turned off at the first gas station she saw. The truck continued down the road. She wanted to tell the driver he'd saved her life, but soon the vehicle was out of sight. Shivering uncontrollably, she rested her head on the steering wheel and said a prayer of thanks.

She found her beige cardigan and her oversized blue cable knit sweater in the trunk of the Honda and pulled them both on.

A balding, middle-aged California Highway Patrol officer walked out of the gas station minimart, heading toward his patrol car. She rushed to him. The Cadillac's driver was still on the summit. Her conscience wouldn't let her leave the man to freeze to death on the mountain.

She told the officer about the Cadillac still on Donner Summit. But not wanting to be held to make a statement, she neglected to mention that she thought the driver had tried to run her off the road.

The patrol car, bar lights flashing, drove out of the gas station heading toward the summit.

From Truckee, it was only about fifteen miles to Tahoe City. However, if it were not for the hope that she'd find her sister at the cabin, she'd stay the night in Truckee.

A sudden chill shook her. She'd left a message on Carrie's cell telling her to go to the cabin. The men who ransacked her house could already be there.

Dear God, don't let me find Carrie in the cabin dead.

Snow concealed the cobblestone driveway to the cabin. No tire tracks, so no one had come to the bungalow since the storm started. Kelly parked in the driveway.

With a sigh of relief, she entered the foyer. Instinctively, she knew the place was empty. Was it that or was it the void death created? Would she find Carrie dead? She shivered.

"Carrie, are you here?"

She searched the house, turning on a light in every room. Memories of the many summers and holidays spent vacationing here filled her. She smiled as she recalled Carrie jumping on the big bed in her grandparent's room. And she thought of stealing downstairs early on Christmas morning to look for Santa. How happy she'd been then and how naive. She pushed down a sob.

What made her life go so wrong? When she left for college, she'd been excited and ready to experience everything life had to offer. Thanks to Johnny Vega, she now knew how cruel and dangerous life could be. A tear slid down her cheek and she wiped it away.

In her grandparent's first-floor bedroom, she turned on the bedside lamp. Too tired to make the bed or change her clothes, she wrapped herself in the queen-size white goose-down comforter and lay down between the Ponderosa posts of the old four-poster bed. She reached over and turned off the lamp.

In the dark, the events on the Donner Pass haunted her. She saw the angry eyes of the man in the Cadillac. Quickly, she replaced it with an image of Brick, his virile male strength and quiet confidence. He'd kept watch over her, protecting her. If only she'd let him come with her because then she wouldn't be alone wondering when the attackers would come to the cabin to kill her.

If she closed her eyes, she could almost hear Brick's breathing, almost sense his vibration and almost feel his touch. *Stop*. He was gone. She'd never see him again.

Chapter 6

Brick watched Kelly's old car pull into the driveway. She was all right. He let his shoulders relax.

The lights of the old home came on one by one. A perfect resort cabin in the woods. Too bad the reality of her situation belied the image. He got out of the vehicle and walked toward the cabin. His boots left a trail in the fresh powder. He checked the perimeter of the place and made sure the first-floor doors and windows were locked.

Back on the auto, he settled in for the night. A thirty-five-millimeter single-lens reflex camera, with a zoom lens, sat in his lap. He patted the nine-millimeter handgun holstered near his heart, then leaned back in the seat.

The weather report said snow flurries throughout the night and set the low temperature at minus five degrees Fahrenheit. He watched the green pine boughs bend under the weight of the falling snow and glisten in the light of the moon.

Waiting sent unnecessary adrenaline flooding through his veins. Stakeouts were a part of his job he could live without. He preferred almost anything except sitting on his butt all night waiting for something to happen, all the while hoping it didn't.

Shattered Rules

Taking off his leather gloves, he blew warm air onto his cold fingers. Kelly would be tucked in bed now, warm and cozy, her shapely lips parted and purring while she slept. He could be in the cabin in a minute and curl up next to her. *Enough.*

His dry throat ached for something hot to drink. He'd stopped at a Seven-Eleven and bought coffee. It'd be cold now in this climate. He took a couple of gulps anyway.

His right leg ached. Taut muscles pulsed around his swollen knee joint. He rubbed it and recalled the ambush that nearly killed him and ended the life of the woman he was guarding.

The FBI had offered him disability retirement. Hell, they'd all but demanded it. He'd refused. With a doctor's okay, he'd fought to be reinstated. Maybe he should've taken early retirement. He could be living in the heat of the Palm Springs desert instead of sitting in a metal box in the middle of a Sierra Nevada snowstorm. He shifted his body to find a more comfortable position in the tight confines of the driver's seat.

He'd endured months of rigorous physical therapy, pushing himself by sheer doggedness. Pain had been a daily annoyance he'd learned to ignore. It was at that time Carrie chose to break their engagement. After that, his dream of returning to work was the only thing that kept him going.

He moved and pain shot through his right knee. That was good. It assured him he wouldn't be comfortable enough to sleep. To protect Kelly, he had to stay awake.

In a nearby pine tree, an owl hooted. He picked up the digital camera and held it to view the area through the zoom lens. Nothing was out of place, only an owl returning from its nightly hunt.

Silence returned. The hours passed slowly, a cold, silent blur of time.

The flurries stopped as the dawn broke. Slowly at first, then with the great force seen in the Sierra Nevada Mountains, the sun pierced the gray mantle of the night.

Brick stretched and twisted the stiffness from his body. While taking a deep breath of the mountain air, he inspected a one-hundred-eighty-degree vista. The grandeur of the Sierras awed him.

The need for hot coffee seized him. He took the camera and stuffed it into his backpack, adjusted the holstered pistol strapped near his left arm, and exited the car.

The key, he'd found earlier, slid into the cabin's front door lock. The weathered door moaned as it opened. In the entryway, he locked the door, and shoved the key in his pocket. Warm air greeted him. He slipped off his snow-covered boots and left them to dry on the green Catalina-tiled foyer.

The thick carpet allowed him to maneuver silently to the great room. He removed the dust cover from a blue velvet sofa positioned at a right angle to a huge river rock fireplace. He winced and then gingerly lowered himself to the sofa, straightened his sore knee in front of him, and sighed. With his parka and backpack on the floor, he adjusted his gun holster to a more comfortable position, leaned back, and closed his eyes. In the familiarity of the old cottage, sleep came easily.

***

A sound signaled an alert in the back of Kelly's mind. Suddenly awake, she strained to see in the low light of dawn and listened for another noise. Her heart pounded so loudly that she didn't know if she would hear anything else. The minutes passed and the silence continued.

Exhaustion overtook fear. She rolled over in bed and closed her eyes.

Later, a ray of light pierced the beveled glass of the bedroom window. She stretched and sat up. What time was it, noon? One? There was no clock in the room.

Still dressed in her jeans and tank top, she got up. A growling stomach and light head warned her she needed to eat. It had been almost two days since she'd had a full meal. What her body needed first was a strong cup of coffee. The last time she was at the cabin she'd left coffee beans in the refrigerator.

On her way to the kitchen, she glanced into the great room and stopped. A man slept on the couch. *Don't panic.* She breathed again. *Brick.*

How did he get in? She'd locked the door. Why was he there? She should demand he tell her why he'd shown up on her doorstep a second time. The truth, she was glad to see him. She believed she'd never hear from him again. After her scare on the road last night, she wanted him nearby.

As he slept, she watched his chest expand, his breathing slow and steady. Her eyes roamed freely over his long frame, stopping at his narrow waist and broad shoulders, and then she looked at the fine structure of his face, chiseled forehead, wide-set eyes, perfectly shaped nose, and high cheekbones. The firm set of his jaw had just a touch of stubble. What would it be like to kiss his full lips?

As if he heard what she was thinking, Brick's eyes flew open.

She jumped. "What are you doing here?" she said to cover her embarrassment.

"I found your extra key. You should know better than to leave a key outside where anyone could find it."

"I didn't ask you how you opened the door. I want to know why you're following me."

He sat up, reached into his pocket, and pulled out the extra key. "Put it somewhere safe."

"Stop ignoring my questions. Why are you here? I haven't seen you for five years and suddenly you show up on my doorstep twice. What's going on?"

His lips formed a firm thin line and anger flickered in his eyes. For the first time since he came back, she was afraid of him. He wasn't the same amiable guy she'd known years earlier. Turbulent undercurrents beat beneath his calm exterior. Which made him the man she needed, a guy strong enough to protect her. All the same, she stepped back from him.

Better change the subject. She cleared her throat. "I was on my way to make coffee. Would you like a cup?"

"Sure."

Their eyes caught and something passed between them, a spark. It sent a potent and enticing sensation through her. She remembered the crush she'd had on him when she was sixteen. What a fool she'd made of herself then, kissing him and telling him she loved him. She hoped he didn't remember.

"I'll see what I can find for breakfast. Give me a few minutes."

"I'll help." He started to get up.

"No. You took care of me yesterday. It's my turn. I'll call you when breakfast is ready."

He smiled and leaned back against the sofa's pillows.

Glad for the opportunity to get away from the heated tension spiraling between them, she ran out of the room.

In the kitchen, she scanned the room. The knotty pine walls had the aroma of the many spices used over the years. They blended into a fragrance that couldn't be manufactured. She was a little girl again in her grandparent's house. It was easy to ignore the rest of the world. She was safe. All was well.

At the kitchen table, she watched Brick push his empty breakfast plate away. "Thanks for the pancakes. It was just what I needed." He looked up from his empty plate. "Always liked this old place. Your granddad built it, right?"

"Yeah." She knew he was making small talk to put her at ease. The least she could do was hold up her end of the conversation. If she pressed for reasons for him being there and angered him, he might leave and she'd be alone again. She shivered at the thought.

"My mom's dad built it. He loved this place and was always working on it. Now the cabin needs repairs, but I'm not handy." She shrugged. "Guess I'll have to learn."

"It'd be a joy to work on a house like this. I could put it back in shape in no time." He cleared his throat. "I don't like the fact Carrie doesn't understand what's happened to you. She could be in danger too. Why don't you phone her again?"

***

Brick watched the sway of Kelly's hips as she left the room. He couldn't believe how sexy she was in the morning, barefoot, hair disheveled, and smelling of soap and pancakes. At breakfast, seeing her lick strawberry preserves from her lips, had almost driven him crazy.

It had taken all his strength of will not to take her in his arms and kiss her lips clean. A hunger and a thirst for Kelly spread through him. He shook his head. It was a hunger that couldn't be filled and a thirst that would never be quenched. If he touched her, the only thing she could do for him was make him lose his FBI career.

Back in the great room, he retrieved his backpack and checked the cell. The battery still held a charge. Time to call his boss, he sat in a leather wing chair, rubbed his painful right knee, and listened to the phone ring.

"Yeah."

"Hey, Don, have anything for me?"

"The intruders were a two-man wrecking crew at the girls' place."

Brick's muscles tightened and his anger flared when he thought of what the men had done to Kelly.

"They were pros," Don added. "They didn't leave anything, no prints, nada. Oh, maybe a couple of hairs. The clean-up crew vacuumed and I'll see what they can find. But unless you have DNA you want to be tested… Finding the men who did this doesn't look good."

"Did you get anything on the car's license number?" He sat up. "Kelly said it was a brown van."

"According to DMV records, that license plate belongs to a subcompact from Merced."

"Damn. The plates were obviously stolen."

"Looks like. Anything on your end?" Don asked.

"Nothing yet." Brick ran his hand over the stubble on his chin and pushed down the annoyance that flared at learning about the license plate. "If I hear anything useful I'll give you a call."

"I'm depending on it."

The phone went dead in his hand.

Shit. It wouldn't hurt Don to say goodbye just once.

Taking a business card out of his wallet, he dialed a company that discreetly took care of houses in need of "special" cleaning. They'd put Kelly's home back in order and save anything that could be salvaged. It wasn't much, but when this was over and he left her, it was one thing she wouldn't have to do.

Shattered Rules

Her perfume permeated the cabin, making it difficult to focus on anything but her. A vision of her disheveled hair and pouting lips heated his blood. The cabin was closing in on him. He paced the room. A good workout would ease his tension. There was no gym in sight and after sitting in the cramped car all night, his sore knee wasn't up to jogging.

A brisk walk around the perimeter of the property would have to do. The Sierra Mountain air would cleanse his blood and clear his mind, then he could concentrate on protecting Kelly.

He left the cabin, locking the front door behind him. No coat was needed, the cold mountain air would do him good.

***

From her grandparent's bedroom, Kelly dialed her sister's cell phone. No answer. She left another message, "Carrie, I know you're busy working, but it's important I talk to you, very important. Call me."

Damn. If everything was okay, she should've heard from her sister by now. Maybe Carrie was just pissed at her. Sisters were supposed to be close; they weren't. Still, Carrie would have called unless—don't go there.

Ever since their parent's death, she and her sister had been at odds. As a teenager, she'd rebelled against Carrie's authority. Even though that was years ago, the relationship hadn't recovered. Now for the first time, she realized her sister hadn't been much older than a teenager when the death of their parents had cast her in the role of stern parent and Kelly in the role of rebellious teen, parts neither had wanted to play.

Again, she prayed Carrie was safe.

The vacation at the cabin had been arranged in the hope that relaxing together and sharing some fun would help their rapport and bring them closer together. She sighed. At this point, she just wanted her sister to be okay.

The faster she got the flash drive from its hiding place and turned it over to Agent Simmons, the sooner she and her sister could get their lives back. When FBI agent Simmons had it, there'd be no reason for anyone to hurt her or Carrie.

At first, she'd resisted the idea of helping Ted Simmons and thought he was crazy. But he'd presented his ID and other undeniable proof of his affiliation with the Bureau. She told him she wasn't a thief. Ted countered by saying that it was Johnny who had stolen the item. Taking it back wasn't a crime; it was for the good of the nation.

How could she say no to the United States government when it needed help? Thousands of innocent people could be hurt if she didn't cooperate. She'd be a traitor if she said no.

Why didn't she ask what was on the flash drive, and then demand answers? Simmons had said it was safer if she didn't comprehend it. *Damn*. She was such a naive little fool.

If she wasn't, she wouldn't have dated Johnny Vega in the first place. A price had to be paid for her stupidity. She just didn't want Carrie to pay for it.

Memories of the men ransacking her home sent tremors down Kelly's spine.

The harsh features of the man driving the Cadillac on Donner Summit came to mind. Something in her memory was trying to get out. Had she seen him before? There was something familiar about him. She knew the man's face. Chilled, she ran out of the room and down the staircase.

Shattered Rules

The kitchen and great room were empty. Movement outside the front window caught her eye. She ran out of the house and down the snow-covered driveway.

"Brick, I remembered something." She jogged to meet him at the end of the driveway.

"Where are your shoes? There's snow on the ground."

She came to a sudden stop and looked down at her pink polished nails peeking through the slush. "I was in a hurry. I didn't think."

"That's your problem. You act before you think."

Annoyed, she concentrated on slowing her breathing. "I wanted to tell you something."

"You'll get frostbite. Tell me when we're back in the house."

Her breath caught when he picked her up and held her to him, his body's heat a counterpoint to the freezing air. With ease, he carried her up the driveway through the open front door and then kicked the door closed.

In the kitchen, he deposited her in the Windsor chair at the table. He yanked a terry dishcloth from the towel bar and tossed it to her. "Dry your feet."

"Don't ever pick me up like that again. I don't appreciate being treated like a child."

"Then don't act like one." His blue eyes flashed as cold as the weather. He turned his back on her.

She swallowed a retort. No point in arguing with him when she needed his help.

He spun around to face her. "What did you remember?"

"Uh."

"You had something to tell me."

She hesitated, then mentioned the Cadillac that almost hit her car and the man who'd promised to kill her.

"At first I thought it was road rage. But now that I've had time to think about it, I realize the driver is a relative of Johnny Vega. His uncle, I think. More than a year ago, I met him at one of Johnny's parties. At the time, I didn't pay attention to him. I only talked to him for a minute. He was nice enough." She shrugged. "He must have been looking for me yesterday. He damn near ran me off the mountain."

"This puts a new complexion on things. I have to know events when they happen. Don't you get that your life's in danger? I came here to protect you. You might have been killed while I was sitting on my ass waiting for you." He stood so quickly that he knocked over the wooden chair, picked it up, and paced the kitchen.

"I shouldn't have let you go by yourself." He frowned. "That's the second time in the last couple of days you might have died. You better get real. I need everything you know. Understand?"

Denial had been her best friend until now. She hadn't believed she could die. At this moment. she did.

With her mouth open to speak, she remembered Agent Ted Simmons warning her to trust only him. The FBI had been infiltrated and even Ted didn't know who he could trust.

"Kelly, what is it?"

"Brick..."

He stared at her with such intensity it shredded her confidence. She turned and left the room.

In her grandparent's bedroom, she lay on the bed. Her headache was back, pounding mercilessly over her right eye. She groaned.

***

Brick watched Kelly run from the kitchen. He shouldn't have yelled at her. She'd been through enough.

The last thing she needed was another man pushing her around. *Damn stupid of you.*

If he was going to keep her safe, he needed to stay cool, be in control, and keep his emotions under wraps. But just now she'd scared the hell out of him. She could be dead on Donner Summit. It was just sheer luck she'd survived.

Old feelings gnawed at him. Five years ago, he'd promised never to let another woman be killed on his watch. The face of Annie, a young government witness he was unable to protect, broke through his memory, her vacant eyes staring at him.

The wind whistled outside the kitchen window. He glanced toward the snow on Donner Summit. The mountain could have been Kelly's burial ground. Fear gripped him. From now, on whatever else happened, he wouldn't fail her.

"I just remembered something."

He glanced up to see her standing in the doorway. Looking frail, she sagged against the door frame.

He fought the urge to comfort her, hold her in his arms. It didn't matter what he needed.

Maybe he should tell her nothing bad would happen to her. No. What good were his promises? He'd vowed to protect Annie and she'd been murdered in front of his eyes. The memory sent a shard of pain running through him.

"Brick."

He yanked his mind to the present. "What do you remember?"

"I have five days to live. If I haven't given the intruders what they want by then, I'm dead." She choked. "They'll find me, wherever I am, and kill me."

Chapter 7

"I don't know why I didn't remember sooner." Kelly collapsed onto a kitchen chair. "A second ago the whole scene played in front of my eyes. I saw the intruder. I heard him threaten me. It was as if he was in the room." She trembled and held on to the table as if it could stop her shaking.

Brick's body went cold. Heat replaced his cold anger as hot fury spiraled in him. "It's okay. When people have a trauma, it's easier for the mind to absorb events if the details come back slowly, a little at a time."

He ached to tell her he'd kill before he let anyone hurt her again. He ached to console her. He ached to caress her. But in the long run, it wouldn't help Kelly and it sure couldn't help his career. It'd only make the future, when they parted, more difficult.

"I shouldn't have yelled at you. Sometimes I'm an insensitive boob," he said.

Their eyes locked and for the first time, she smiled. "Insensitive boobs are people too."

He laughed out loud. Even under hellish circumstances, she had a sense of humor.

"I could drive you to a safe house. You could stay there until I locate Johnny Vega and the men who attacked you."

"I can't." She pushed her hair out of her eyes and leaned forward in the chair. "Carrie is still out there alone. Going to a safe house won't protect her. And I have something else I've got to do. I have to go to Reno. You can come with me if you want to. But, with or without you, I'm going." She stared at him and he saw her steely determination.

He might force her into a safe house. Drag her there by her hair if needed. Instead, he said, "Okay, let's go to Reno."

***

Hard to believe there'd been a snowstorm yesterday. Kelly leaned back in Brick's passenger seat. The car's plush leather was comfortable and the sun filtered through the closed car windows, heating the interior. For the first time in hours, she felt warm. Tension melted from her muscles and she calmed down.

With a serious expression, Brick stared at the road ahead. His powerful hands squeezed the steering wheel so tightly she feared it might crack. His well-honed muscles were taught. She sensed his stress. It filled the car's interior. He glanced at her. She was chilled by the fierceness of his eyes. She turned away.

He must have other responsibilities that needed his attention. Why was he still with her? What was he thinking? He probably had a family waiting for him. For all she knew, he was married and had children. It'd been almost five years since she'd seen him. There'd certainly been enough time for him to have a family.

She pictured him with another woman. A wave of envy towards the unknown female shocked her. There was no wedding ring on his ring finger. Still, many married men don't wear a wedding band.

Maybe he was angry at her for keeping him from his family. *Stop.* His personal life was none of her business. She must remember that. Today he was with her offering protection. After the ransacking of her house and her scare on Donner Pass, she needed him. Grateful for his help, she'd take it for as long as it was offered. However, she had no right to pry into his private life.

She took a quick deep breath and watched the mountain's scenery rush by.

They stopped at a truck stop on the outskirts of Reno. With his mobile phone, she looked up the address of a wig shop.

Forty-five minutes later, she was a brunette. She pulled at the straight brown hair that ended just below her chin. Even though the wig was too dark for her pale skin, she definitely didn't look like the blonde she saw in the mirror every morning.

"I want to go to my dorm room, south campus, Juniper Hall."

"That might be the first place the intruders would look for you."

"They don't know about the place. I haven't been there in months. Not since I first met Johnny. I left something. I need it."

Brick grunted, then drove toward the campus.

Her roommate, Amanda, answered the door, with maroon hair, multi-pierced ears, and a nose ring glistening in the sun. Her nails were painted black and so were her lips. A spider web with a Monarch Butterfly trapped in it was tattooed on her upper right arm. She was dressed in a black ball gown as a woman might dress if she were waiting to appear in a goth video. Kelly smiled at the surprised look on Brick's face when he saw her. To his credit, he didn't say anything. He waited at the open front door.

"Kelly is that you? What's up with the wig?"

"It's a long story. I'll tell you later. I'm kind of in a hurry."

"Whatever." Amanda shrugged.

In her old room, Kelly watched dust bunnies run over forgotten textbooks. An unmade bed sat waiting against the wall.

She sat in a wooden chair and pulled open the desk drawer. Inside there were a few pens and an unsharpened pencil. She yanked out the drawer and turned it over letting the items in the drawer fall to the floor.

The envelope she'd taped there was gone and in its place was a note from Amanda. "I took the cash. I owe you three hundred dollars. I needed to pay rent."

Shit. That was her traveling money. Yet, she shouldn't blame Amanda. After all, she'd left to go live with Johnny without giving Amanda any notice or a chance to get another roommate.

The money she'd had in her wallet was stolen by the intruders. "Damn," she whispered in frustration.

When she came out of the bedroom she forced a smile.

"Ready to go?" Brick said.

"I guess so. I just don't know where to go or what to do next."

"First we'll get a room here on campus at the University Inn." He took her arm. "Tonight, we'll go to the Big Top Casino."

"Are you coming back? Or do I need to get another roommate?"

"I don't know, Amanda. I'll let you know."

"Rent's due in a couple of weeks."

"I know. I'll talk to you before that. I promise."

***

Amanda stared out of the front window and watched Kelly and the guy leave. Then she walked to the nearby table where there was a landline phone. Moving her purse and keys out of the way, she searched for her old paper address book. She retrieved the phone number she wanted and called it.

"Hey, this is Amanda, Kelly's roommate. She was here."

"When?" The male voice asked.

"She just left and she wasn't alone. There was this hunk with her, a total hunk."

"Who was he?"

"He didn't say. A boyfriend I guess."

"Police?"

"No way, but he was big enough to be a Marine. Tall, I mean way tall, a hunk, rad looking, blonde hair, and really cool blue eyes."

"What's his name?"

"He didn't tell me. But you want to know something weird?"

"Yeah."

"Kelly was wearing a short brown wig. I mean if I had natural blonde hair you wouldn't catch me in a mousy brown wig. Go figure."

"Anything else?"

"She wore jeans and a green Oakland A's sweatshirt. I mean really. It's so sad. She used to care about her appearance."

"Did you see their car?"

"The guy must be doing okay cause he's driving a Volvo."

"You saw the car?"

"Yeah, it's gray."

"Did you get the license?"

"Uh, no."

"What did they want?"

"She didn't say. But she was looking for something."

"What?"

"Don't know, but I've got their cell phone number."

"Give it?"

Amanda told him the number.

"So far you haven't given me anything I can use. I don't pay for useless information," he said gruffly.

She didn't like his tone of voice, but his cash was good money. "I heard them say they were going to get a room at the University Inn and then go to the Big Top casino tonight. That's all. Look, man, I called like you wanted. I want my money."

"Did you tell them about me?"

"No, of course not. What could I tell? I don't know anything and I don't want to know. I just want my money. It's time to pay for tuition, so, I got to have it!"

"Watch your post office box."

"Okay, good."

"Call me if you hear from them again."

The connection went dead.

"Jerk!" A twinge of guilt ran through her after informing on Kelly. She dismissed it. *Damn, the college for taking my grants away when they've just raised tuition.*

She shouldn't feel guilty. She didn't owe Kelly anything. The girl was only a random chick who happened to end up as her roommate. If she could make a few bucks off her, so much the better.

That's what she told herself, but a shiver went through her. She locked the front door and rubbed her arms for warmth against a sudden chill.

***

Spring semester was over and the summer session hadn't started yet. The University Inn had rooms available. Brick registered and got one for each of them.

They were on the third floor, directly across the hall from each other. Though he didn't think anyone would know they were at the inn, he wanted her nearby, but not too close. For her protection from him, there'd be no adjoining rooms. Her proximity wasn't making it easy to keep his hands off her. He needed the cold light of the hallway between them.

He had an errand to run and asked her to stay in the room until he got back, then drove out of the lot and parked on the street. He watched to see if she would do what she was told this time.

After thirty minutes, he dialed her room. She answered. He hung up.

He called his boss. "Don, anything new on your end?"

"Old man Vega, Johnny's grandfather and leader of the Vega crime family, is dying. Rumor has it he's about to name a successor. A lot of guys want the job, but Johnny wants it more. Talk is he's planning something big to get his granddad's attention."

"What does this have to do with Kelly?"

"Good question. I was hoping you could tell me. She's Johnny's girlfriend. Maybe she's helping him plan his ascent to the top of the Vega crime family," Don said.

"Not likely."

"How do you know? She sure as hell wouldn't tell you."

Brick bit back a caustic response. "I know everything that has happened recently."

"She might be holding back."

He bristled at Don's words, yet he'd had similar thoughts. If it were anyone except her, he might believe she'd lied. But not Kelly, he knew her. And he'd seen the bruises on her arm, the terror in her eyes, and her bewildered expression as she tried to understand what was happening. She'd been completely truthful with him. He'd have trouble believing otherwise.

"You haven't seen her in five years. People change, and they get desperate. They do things you'd never think they would. She's not the sweet young thing you remember," Don continued.

"Kelly is not involved with Vega's business. She's a kid who got mixed up with the wrong guy."

"Just keep your eyes open and stay in touch." His boss ended the call.

The thought of Carrie's little sister being involved with the Vega family's business turned Brick's stomach. He considered it for a moment. No. He didn't believe it. Yet he'd been deceived before, fooled by his partner, a best friend, and the man he trusted with his life. Because of that, the witness he'd been protecting was murdered and he'd nearly died along with her. His shattered knee was a reminder of his failure to see a friend's treason and every day he lived with that incompetence.

The doctors had put his shattered knee back together. Putting his life back together had been harder. While he lay in the hospital bed wondering if he would lose his leg, Carrie returned his engagement ring. To her credit, she had cried and said he deserved someone a better person.

In order to keep his job, his superiors made him go see a shrink. The doctor had told him not to let a single act of betrayal color his whole life. That advice had stuck in his throat, but he'd forced himself to swallow. Finally, he was allowed to return to work.

Now he was reliving his partner's betrayal. The treacherous friend had been right beside him smiling at him. Why hadn't he known? There must've been signs, but he hadn't seen them. If he had, Annie, the woman he was assigned to protect, would still be alive and Carrie would be his wife.

Another thing the doctor said came to mind. The past cannot be changed. Living had to be done in the present. He could create a better future by letting go of the past and living in the present, one day at a time. That was good advice too. Except Kelly was part of his past. Though he didn't want to, he was being forced to live with her.

He returned with just enough time to get back to the University Inn for a shower and a shave before dinner.

Maybe he should leave Kelly at the Inn while he went to The Big Top alone. Nope, he didn't like the idea of her being out of his sight. She was safer with him.

Chapter 8

The Big Top casino, a beige monolith with a twenty-seven-floor tower, looked like a castle, with a blacktop parking lot as its moat.

When Kelly walked into a gaming room, it was as if she had entered a live video game, with loud music, flashing lights, bright colors, and ringing bells. Throngs of people, in various styles of casual dress, moved in all directions.

Fear rippled through her. What if someone recognized her? She tugged on her wig. It pinched her scalp. She adjusted it and hoped none of her blonde hair had poked out at the back.

Brick stood next to her watching the scene before them. Since he'd picked her up for dinner, his behavior toward her had changed. His manner was more reserved. During the ride to the casino, she'd tried to engage him in conversation, with little result. She shouldn't take it personally. He must have a lot on his mind. There was no way to know what other pressure he might be under. Again, she reminded herself whether she liked it or not, his personal life was none of her business.

He led her to the first-floor lounge, a bustling enterprise filled with patrons. They found seats at the bar and he ordered two cokes.

"Drink it. You need the caffeine to stay awake. It could be a long night."

She didn't usually drink soda, but since it was for medicinal purposes, she sipped the caffeine-riddled drink. Too sweet, she should've told him to get a diet cola.

He gulped down his drink. "Wait here, I'm going to talk to some of the hotel staff."

He didn't wait for her to answer. It was an official order. She watched him leave, his broad shoulders back, his head high and his ass tight.

The crowds increased. The decibel level rose in the bar. Forty minutes went by and he didn't return. A man in ill-fitting jeans and a white T-shirt checked her out. He came close and was about to speak but belched instead, spewing alcohol breath in her direction.

A grin spread across his face. "Mind if I join you, little lady?" He sat on the bar stool next to hers.

She turned her back on him.

"Okay, girly, I can take a hint." He belched again. "There are lots of girls around here who want my company," he yelled. "I sure as hell don't need you."

People in the bar stared at her, some sympathetic, some disgusted. A young blonde woman walked by and the man stumbled off his bar stool and followed her. A pang of sympathy for the unknown woman shook Kelly.

If FBI Agent Ted Simmons hadn't talked her into taking the damn flash drive in the first place, she wouldn't be sitting in a bar being harassed by a drunk.

She hissed under her breath. How long was she supposed to sit on her butt and wait for Brick?

Shattered Rules

Agent Simmons had mentioned that he worked undercover as a waiter in this casino. Was he here now? If she could find him, she could end this mess tonight. She'd take him to the hidden flash drive. It would be hard to get there at night. Still, she'd do it.

With a sip of her soda, she made up her mind to find Ted Simmons.

"Can I get you another one?" the bartender asked.

"No thanks. I'm leaving, but if the guy that was with me returns, please tell him I'll meet him in the car."

She smiled her best sexy smile and hoped that would help the bartender remember her. He nodded and went to serve his other customers.

An open hallway led to the gaming rooms. Herds of people mingled in the space. Jostled by the crowds, she weaved in and out of the throngs. The multitudes closed in on her. Panic rose as she sensed someone was watching her. The intruder had said he'd find her anywhere. She pulled on her wig and pushed back the blond hair that threatened to peek out. She quickly moved out of the room and down a hallway.

Customers flowed in both directions and she peered at their faces hoping to find Agent Simmons among them. In a gaming room, a man collided with her as he jockeyed for position at a corner slot machine. The noise grew louder and the flashing lights and ringing bells set her nerves on edge.

After finding a bank of elevators, she pressed the up arrow. A few seconds later, one arrived, the door opened and the elevator emptied. She entered. Two people were still in the elevator, but she didn't look at them.

She pushed a button for the twenty-fifth floor. A lounge and a restaurant with a view of the city were on the floor. She thought Simmons worked there. Even if he didn't, it'd be a relief to get away from the crush of people on the first floor.

What was the name Simmons was using? He'd told her once. Craig something, Craig Fletcher, he told her to ask for that name if she needed to call him at the casino.

The four-star restaurant was buzzing as the waiters moved quickly around the window-flanked room. She told the maître d' she wanted to see Craig Fletcher.

"You just missed him," he said. "Gone home early. A family emergency or something. You can leave a message if you want."

"Uh, no thank you." A message couldn't help now.

What kind of an emergency had called him away from the casino? Was it a family problem or was it the FBI summoning him with new orders? There was no way to know. She'd have to wait for their planned meeting. Her body trembled as she fought disappointment. She pushed the button and waited to be taken back to the first floor.

She entered the empty elevator. The doors were about to close when a masculine hand wearing a gold and black ring with an initial "N" on it, stopped them. A man pulled the doors open and she stared into the eyes of the intruder, the one who had kissed her and hurt her. She quickly gazed down at her feet. When she looked up again, he had turned his back on her.

The elevator continued its descent. Bile rose in her throat and she held her hand to her mouth. Her chest heaved and she took a controlled breath. Because of her disguise, he didn't recognize her. Nonetheless, he must have felt her staring at him because he turned and said, "Yo, bitch, what you lookin at?"

"Nothing," her voice squeaked. Just then, the elevator doors opened, and a woman with three noisy kids charged into the elevator. She used the opportunity to rush out of the doors before they closed.

In the hallway, she gulped for air and tried to stop shaking. What floor was she on?

Calm down. This time she wasn't trapped in her home and at the mercy of the intruder. Even though the man saw her, the wig kept him from recognizing her. All she had to do was find an exit and go back to the car.

She walked quickly down the corridor looking for an exit sign. She found one and turned toward it.

The hair on the back of her neck rose. Someone was following her, a man of average height, brown hair, and brown eyes. He was well dressed in a flashy kind of way with a brightly multicolored silk shirt, green pants, and shiny black leather shoes.

Just a patron of the hotel, that's what she told herself, but she didn't buy it. Her back muscles tightened and instincts told her this man was trouble. A phony smile spread across his face and his dark eyes narrowed when he said, "You're Kelly."

He must've seen the fear in her eyes because he said, "Relax honey, nobody's going to hurt you."

"How do you know my name?"

"Carrie told me. Come on we'll get a drink. I'll tell you all about it." He sent another insincere grin in her direction.

No one should've recognized her. Her sister wouldn't have given her a second glance. Earlier, when she looked in the mirror, she didn't even recognize herself.

He walked toward her.

How close was the exit? Maybe she could sprint to it before he knew what she was doing. She turned to look. The hall ended a few yards behind her. No exit. She must have made a wrong turn.

She took two steps back from him. He matched her footsteps for footsteps. Shortly, she'd be trapped at the end of the hall. She stopped.

He did too. "Come on, I'm buying. I'll tell you all about how I met your sister." A smile formed on his thin lips.

Maybe he did know Carrie, knew where she was. He could explain why her sister hadn't answered her cell phone. She wanted to believe the man but didn't.

"Let's go," he said as if he were talking to a young child. "Honey, I'm not going to bother you. I just want to talk," his voice warm as a gentle southern breeze.

When she didn't move, his brown eyes narrowed and his hands flexed to form fists. "Come here." He stood in the middle of the hall. "You're going with me one way or the other." Anger flashed in his eyes and his once smiling lips formed a straight line. "Why not make it easy on yourself?" He held out his hand.

He outweighed her by at least fifty pounds and she couldn't get by him. He'd grab her. Still, there was no way she was willingly going with him.

"Okay, the hard way."

If she could kick him in just the right spot, she'd disable him long enough to get away. Surprise was on her side. Adrenaline rushed through her veins. She forced a smile on her trembling lips. Her hands tingled and her heart pounded so hard she wanted to press her hand against her chest to slow it down.

"I'll come." She took a step toward him.

"That's right, honey." For the first time, his smile appeared sincere.

She inched forward. The trick was to be close enough for her foot to have maximum power, but not so near he could grab her. A tepid smile was the best she could manage as she moved toward him.

When he opened his mouth to speak, she kicked with all her strength and felt a jarring thud as her foot connected with his solar plexus. A look of surprise crossed his face. He grunted and dropped to the floor. He grimaced in pain and his angry eyes tracked her, but he didn't move.

Nausea filled her as she sprinted by him. She'd never hurt anyone before.

The exit door was at the other end of the hallway. She pushed it open and ran down six flights of stairs. On the bottom floor, she stopped, gasped for air, and tried to slow her breathing.

The exit door slammed and she heard footsteps running down the staircase. It had to be the stranger. In a second he'd find her.

Dashing outside into the dim light of the parking lot, she searched for Brick's car.

The sound of a closing door echoed in her ears. The man was outside too.

"Kelly, where are you?"

His gruff voice sent a chill through her. She heard his footfall coming in her direction. The soles of his shoes slapped on the blacktop as he ran toward her.

"Kelly."

She rushed around the corner of the building near the casino kitchen's back door. She pulled on the door handle. Locked, she pounded her fists against the door.

"Kelly, I'm coming for you."

Two large dumpsters, one filled with empty boxes, the other overflowing with kitchen waste, stood by the locked kitchen door.

She forced her body into the small space between the two garbage bins, breathed in the smell of decaying food and almost gagged.

"I know you're out there," he said, panting as he caught his breath.

He stood beside the bin. If he came any closer, he'd see her. She struggled to stop her trembling.

"You better answer me, because I'm getting pissed."

The sound of blood rushing through her veins was so loud she thought he'd hear it.

"Answer, bitch, cause I'm startin to be real mad and you don't want to see what I can do when I'm angry."

She squeezed her eyes shut and waited, imagining what he might do to her when he found her.

***

Brick re-entered the bar where he'd left Kelly. She was nowhere to be seen. He should've known she wouldn't do what he told her to do. "Damn," he said under his breath.

He motioned to the bartender. The man walked leisurely in his direction. "I was here a few minutes ago with a young woman. Any chance you saw which way she went?"

"The pretty brunette with the amazing eyes?"

Brick paused imperceptibly. "Yeah, that's the one." It was hard to think of Kelly as a brunette.

"She went back to the car."

"Thanks." Brick left a big tip on the bar.

In the parking lot, he found the Volvo and peered into the interior. Empty.

"Hell!"

Where could she be? Why didn't Kelly ever follow simple directions?

He went back into the casino.

Chapter 9

Kelly stared into the darkness as cold terror saturated her. He was close enough to touch the dumpster. In a moment the man would grab her.

"You hear me, Ho? When I get my hands on you…"

She didn't move, didn't breathe.

"Damn, you!" His curse filled the still night air.

She sucked in a bit of air and held her breath again.

"Frigging bitch!" He slammed his hand on the metal dumpster.

The vibration shook her. *Don't panic. Hold on. Stay calm.*

The man hit the garbage bin again. "Bitch, where the hell did you go?" Finally, his footsteps moved away from her hiding place.

When a door slammed, she exhaled and took a deep breath. As quietly as possible, she squeezed out from between the dumpsters and gasped for air.

She stumbled toward the parking lot. Where was the car? She jogged up and down the aisles, Brick's car nowhere in sight. She was about to give up and go back into the casino when an immense van pulled out of a parking space. The Volvo was parked next to it and now in full view. She ran toward it.

The car was empty. Where was Brick? He should be there waiting for her. Had someone waylaid him too?

Thank God he'd left the car unlocked. She got into the back and this time locked the doors. She lay down on the seat and hoped the car looked empty to the casual viewer.

How long should she wait for Brick?

***

"Open the door." Brick knocked on the car's window. Kelly startled.

"Where the hell have you been? I went back to the bar and you were gone. I've looked all over the damn building for you," he hissed.

"Where have *you* been? I waited for almost an hour in the bar. How long was I supposed to wait, all night?"

"When I tell you to wait, you stay until I get back."

"You can't tell me what to do."

"Look. I was worried about you." His expression softened. "When you weren't in the bar and you weren't in the car, I didn't know what to think. If I'm going to have a chance of keeping you safe, I need to know where you are all the time."

"It's very annoying when you're right." She paused. "I should've stayed in the bar."

He shrugged. "I had a good lead, but it turned out to be a wild goose chase. Are you okay? Did something happen while I was gone?"

"Yeah." She tried to swallow the lump that filled her throat.

"Tell me while we drive."

She crawled into the front passenger's seat.

"Buckle up," he said as he drove out of the parking lot.

Shattered Rules

A few blocks down the road, he drove into a gas station and parked next to a gas pump. "Never know when we're going to need a full tank."

She followed him out of the car. Tired and at the same time restless, she stretched while he filled the gas tank.

"I'm going into the station and pay with cash. No point in leaving a credit card trail for someone to follow."

She paced in front of the station.

A truck pulled into the lot and a teenager jumped out and ran into the store. A bald man and his Golden Retriever jogged by on the street. A woman talking on a phone waited at a bus stop. Surrounded by urban life, it felt good to be anonymous, only another person in a sea of people, all on a mission to fulfill their special needs and meet their hidden desires.

The whoosh of car tires on the pavement drew her attention, vehicles taking people out to have a good time or home to get ready for the next day's work. It all appeared so normal. For a moment she felt a part of that normalcy, instead of a confused player in an odd game of hide and seek.

In the dark, she watched Brick through the gas station's window. He casually chatted with the young female cashier. With a friendly smile on his face, no one would suspect he had a care in the world. A twinge of envy pinched Kelly. He never smiled like that when he looked at her. She noticed desire in the young woman's bright eyes.

His carefree "nice guy" demeanor disappeared and a serious one reappeared when he exited the store. His intense eyes were Sapphire in the low light. She watched him scan the parking lot and the street beyond.

He moved toward her. "You better tell me what happened at the casino."

She hesitated, not wanting to relive the fear she experienced moments earlier. The words were forced from her tightened throat.

Without interrupting, he listened.

She expected his anger, but when she finished, he said, "We better get rid of the wig and sweatshirt. They aren't going to protect you now."

She'd gotten herself in trouble because she didn't stay in the bar and wait for him. Still, she was relieved not to receive his reprimand as she'd expected.

She tugged off the wig and shook her head to let her blonde hair fall free. "You paid so much for this." She waved the hairpiece. "Wish I could return it." She paused. "I'll pay you back."

"Don't worry about it. Throw it away, the sweatshirt too. Three points, if you make it in the trashcan from where you stand."

She smiled, thankful he was making light of the situation. His anger was more than she could handle right now.

The sweatshirt slipped easily into the trashcan, followed by the wig. Adjusting a strap on her cotton tank top, she hoped the night air didn't get any colder.

"The attacker in the casino was obviously given a detailed description of your disguise." He ran his hand across his jaw. "You were lucky there was only one guy after you or the outcome might have been different."

"You're scaring me again."

"Good. Next time don't go off on your own."

"How did the guy find me? Who told him what I look like? No one knows me as a brunette. Even my sister wouldn't recognize me." Kelly paused. "Amanda."

"Right."

"Why would she do it?"

76

"Maybe we should go ask her."

"Now? It must be 10:30 at night."

"No time like the present. We might get more answers if she's not expecting us."

"True, but—" She let her voice dwindle into silence. Completely exhausted, the thought of another confrontation was more than she wanted to contemplate. She hadn't recovered from her earlier encounter. All she wanted to do was go back to her room and sleep.

Brick put his arm around her and pulled her close. "I know you're tired, but we need to do this."

She let her head rest on his chest, grateful for his warmth and strength. His rough hand gently caressed her cheek. She reached for it and pressed her lips into the palm of his hand. He sucked in a breath of air and let her go.

She shivered in the night air.

"You've been through enough. You should be home in bed. But I don't think Amanda will open the door if I show up alone." He lifted her face to his. "You don't have to say anything. Just stand next to me."

His lips opened slightly, tormenting her. It'd be so easy to kiss him, but when he said she should be in bed, he didn't mean in his bed. She sighed.

***

It was almost eleven o'clock by the time they reached the university, but the campus still hummed with activity. Students milled around outside the buildings and music blared from the dorm rooms' open windows. Laughter filled the night.

At that moment, Kelly realized what an idiot she'd been, never understanding how good she'd had it at college. She should have stayed in school and not taken the job at the casino. Then she'd never have met Johnny Vega. *Too late now.*

Amanda's apartment was dark when they reached it.

"Kelly, do you have your key?"

"I didn't think I'd need it. I left it in Palo Alto."

Brick knocked on the door, softly at first and then harder. No answer.

"Does the apartment have a landline?"

"Yeah."

"What's the number?"

She told him and he called it on his cell. She could hear the phone ringing inside the apartment, but no one answered, not even the message machine picked up. Do you know Amanda's cell?"

"I never had a reason to call her."

"I'm going in. Stand guard and let me know if anyone comes by."

"That's breaking and entering."

"I'm not breaking in. I have a key."

"What?"

He pulled a little metal box from his pocket and held it up for her to see. It looked like it was filled with Paraffin and she could see several impressions of keys in the wax. He put it back into his pants pocket.

"When we were here today and you went to your room, Amanda followed and watched you from the doorway. I saw her keys on the desk and took impressions. This afternoon, I had keys made."

"Standard FBI breaking and entering technique?"

"It's not standard or FBI, but I've found it useful."

Before she could respond, he entered the apartment and closed the door behind him.

What would she say to Amanda if she came home while Brick was in the apartment?

78

Shattered Rules

She couldn't think of a single believable excuse for him being in the apartment. She glanced down at the lit parking lot. Amanda's car wasn't there.

After a while, he came out carrying a small plastic wastebasket.

"Why are you taking her trash?" she whispered.

"You'd be surprised what a person's trash can tell you. She won't miss it. Her closet and dresser drawers are empty. She packed and flew the coop. From the look of it, she left in a big hurry."

"I can't believe it. She told me she wanted to keep the apartment for another year. What could've made her leave?"

He shrugged. "Let's get back to the Inn and see what clues she's left for us."

At the University Inn, Brick walked to her door.

"Kelly, you look tired. I'll check out Amanda's trash in my room. Get a good night's sleep. I'll see you in the morning,"

"Okay." She unlocked her door and started to enter.

"Remember to lock your door." He smiled.

"Night." She smiled back and closed the door.

Total exhaustion hit her as she entered. The bedroom was dark, but the bathroom light was on. She must have forgotten to turn it off when she left. It didn't matter. She needed an aspirin anyway. Her headache was back.

In the bright light of the bathroom, she found the painkiller in the medicine cabinet and gulped down two tablets. She ran a brush through her tangled hair. She should shower and wash her hair, but she was too exhausted. Tomorrow would be time enough.

A noise in the bedroom startled her. "Brick?" She rushed into the room and flicked on the overhead light.

Someone grabbed her.

Chapter 10

Kelly fought the man who seized her, but he held her tight, his hand over her mouth. "Scream and I'll slit your throat."

He wore a mask. Still, she recognized his voice, overpowering cologne and cigarette breath, the intruder from her house. She twisted in his arms, trying to loosen his grip. His hold tightened and she saw his signet ring.

"Do you have it?"

"No," She choked on the word.

"Get it. You don't have much time left. I'll be back. If you don't have it then, you're dead." He threw her to the floor and ran out of the room.

The slam of the door reverberated in her head. She sat up slowly and rubbed her arms. As her eyes adjusted to the bright light of the room, she noticed bedding was strewn on the floor and the chairs were knocked over. The mattress was on the floor too. The few items she brought with her were thrown in all directions. "Not again. Not again." She groaned.

Someone knocked.

"Kelly, you still up?"

"Brick?" She scrambled to her feet and yanked the door open.

"I forgot to tell you what time..." Brick's eyes darkened as he scanned the ransacked room. "Damn! Are you okay?"

"Did you see anyone in the hall?"

"No." He came to her and held her to him.

"A guy was here when I came back into the room. He's gone."

"Did you recognize him?"

"It all happened so fast and he was wearing a mask. But I know it was one of the men who ransacked my house." She rubbed her arms again.

"Is anything missing?"

"I don't know." She stepped away from him and examined the room. "I didn't bring very much with me." She hesitated. "The intruder found me just like he said he would. Oh God, what am I going to do?" She swallowed a sob.

"Calm down. We don't know if this attack has anything to do with you. It could be a simple break-in."

"No. They told me they could find me anytime, anywhere. This is their way of proving it." Her body tensed ready to bolt, but where could she run? "This isn't right. They can't do this to me." Anger replaced her fear. "Somehow I'm going to stop them."

"Let's not jump to any conclusions. This is a university. Lots of mischief happens on campus," he said, his voice composed.

"First I was attacked in the casino and now here in the hotel. How did the men know how to find me?"

His expression turned grim. She could tell by his expression he thought it was one of the intruders too, but for her sake, he was putting a better face on things.

"If they wanted to frighten me, they've succeeded."
She gazed at the ransacked room. "I can't stay here. I've got to get out—now."

"Maybe that's what they want. They could be outside watching, hoping you'll run."

"Then what should I do? I'm so exhausted. I can't think."

He extended his hand to her. She went to him and he held her. Electricity flowed through him, arcing to her, giving her strength.

"They knew you were here because of Amanda."

"Why would she do that? I've never done anything to hurt her."

"For one of the oldest reasons in the world, money."

"What kind of world are we living in?" she said, not expecting an answer.

She moved out of his arms and began to pick up her possessions.

"Kelly, whoever did this is gone. Let's get some sleep. Tomorrow everything will look better."

"Maybe." She picked up a black bra from the floor. "But I can't sleep here. I'm sorry. I just can't."

"Okay, finish packing." He picked up a few items and handed them to her. Then he righted the furniture and set the mattress back on the box spring. "That's good enough. Let's get the hell out of here."

They walked across the hall to his room and turned on the light. His clothes had been dumped on the floor, the mattress was overturned and the desk chair was upside down.

The message was clear. She understood the men who ransacked her room were warning him as well. They recognized he was with her and they could get to him too.

A surge of adrenaline raced through her. They'd kill Brick and Carrie and it would be her fault.

A slight tremor shook her and she leaned against a wall for support. She choked back fear and glanced at Brick's stoic expression.

"We have to leave this place," she whispered.

He picked up his belongings and tossed them into his backpack and put the contents of Amanda's wastebasket into a plastic laundry bag he found in the closet.

"Whoever did this didn't take anything. It was just a scare tactic." He zipped his backpack shut.

"Well, it worked. I'm scared as hell." She held her arms around her midriff in an attempt to stop her trembling. "What are we going to do now?"

"I'll think of something."

She wanted him to promise everything was going to be okay and there'd be no more of these kinds of incidents. *He can't.*

"Okay, we're out of here." He picked up his belongings and led her out the door.

"Going where?"

"Do you like movies?"

"What an odd question. Of course, I do. Why?"

"I saw a flyer in the lobby for an all-night drive-in movie theater. Have you ever been to one?"

"No."

"I have when I was a kid. I went with my grandparents." He smiled. "I didn't think there were any left. You'll like it."

"The men might be watching for us. How can we get out without being seen?"

"I have a plan.

In the hallway, Brick punched the button to call the elevator.

"Kelly, when the elevator gets here go in and keep the door open. I'll be right back."

From the open elevator door, she watched him as he set off the fire alarm. He ran and slid through the doors just before they closed. The car automatically returned to the first floor and opened into the lobby.

"If someone is watching the hotel, we're going to give him a show."

Before she could respond, he grabbed her by the hand and pulled her to the back of the hotel lobby.

The alarm continued to sound.

"We'll wait for the fire trucks to arrive," he said as he glanced out of the hotel window.

Just then, the loudspeaker blared, "Please evacuate your room. This is not a drill. Leave your room immediately. Do not use the elevator. Use the stairs to exit. This is not a drill." Then the announcement repeated.

Blurry-eyed people, in various states of dress, rushed down the stairs and stumbled into the lobby.

"I'm sorry we scared them. They look frightened," Kelly whispered. "Couldn't we tell them there's no fire?"

Brick glanced at her but didn't answer.

"I'm being foolish, but I understand what it's like to have fear change your life."

Brick's expression softened. He squeezed her hand and then released it.

The noise in the lobby swelled and the hotel guests surrounded the front desk. She watched the night manager, standing behind the desk, trying to calm the patrons as they asked questions all at once.

"The fire department has been called. Everything is under control," the manager shouted over the din of the questions. "I don't know what floor the fire started on, but the fire trucks will be here in no time. I suggest everyone wait in the parking lot until the fire department tells us it is okay to return to the building. Do not go back to your rooms."

Brick pulled her into the center of the people in the lobby. "When we exit the building, don't run. I don't want to call attention to us," he whispered in her ear. "Walk slowly out of the building with the group and go to the car. I'll be right beside you."

She nodded and they moved with the crowd toward the backdoor.

The fire alarm continued to blare. A fire truck's siren sounded and a hook and ladder truck pulled up in front of the building just as they left the lot. She looked back. Cars drove out of the parking lot and turned left and right.

"The patrons probably expect flames to erupt from the Inn at any moment."

"Put your head down. If anyone is watching, I want this car to look like there's only one person in it."

"Where are we going?"

"The University Drive-In. They're showing a Hitchcock retrospective. I saw the poster in the lobby."

"You can't be serious."

***

Vehicles rushed out of the parking lot as the fire department set up roadblocks in front of the University Inn. The intruder lost sight of the Volvo. Fisting his hands, he let out a string of expletives in his native language. He twisted the gold and onyx ring on his finger while he considered what to do next.

He'd drive around town on the off chance he would see the car Kelly's friend was using.

An hour later, he realized how many gray Volvos there were in town, but not the right one. Frustrated, he parked the rental truck near Amanda's motel room. If he couldn't find Kelly, he'd get Amanda. If the roommate thought she could hide from him, she was a fool. Earlier, before he went to the Inn, he'd followed her to this rundown motel. With a little persuasion, he could find out if she'd held back any information from him. He smiled. It would be fun to make her give it up.

He took off his signet ring and scratched his red-blistered fingers. "Nerves," the doctors had told him. His hands itched because of nervous stress. He dug his nails into his flesh. The pain was better than the itch that was driving him crazy.

The doctor had told him to choose a different line of work, something that didn't cause so much stress. Then the dermatologist prescribed a cortisone cream. The intruder laughed. The Doc would be alarmed if he knew what he did for a living. He scratched his hands until they bled and put his ring back on his reddened finger.

***

It was after midnight when Brick and Kelly found the drive-in movie theater. The retrospective had just started. In a huge parking lot, rows of cars and trucks faced an enormous movie screen. It was an old-fashioned drive-in with metal posts in each parking space, holding a speaker for the vehicle. The speaker would be put in the window so each auto could adjust the sound to the liking of the passengers.

"There aren't many places like this left in the world," he said. "It's good the place is so busy. We can hide in plain sight."

He found a parking space in the middle of the fourth row. The movie screen loomed high in front of the car. The opening credits of "The Birds" rolled before her eyes.

Vehicles were parked on both sides of Brick's car. The one on the left appeared to be empty. The sedan on the right held two people, kissing furiously, their bodies intertwined.

He grunted and turned away from them, trying to ignore the sounds of their lovemaking.

"Kelly, think you can get some rest?"

"I'm so tired I could sleep anywhere. Anywhere but the University Inn."

"Good. Why don't you crawl into the back seat and sleep?"

Using his backpack as a pillow, she lay down and closed her eyes.

He watched the frames of the movie play in front of him, but his mind was elsewhere. Two days had passed and he'd learned nothing that could help the FBI or Kelly. Someone was one step ahead of him. For her sake, he'd tried not to show his frustration, but it was eating at him.

He could use help, but at this point in the investigation, he didn't want to bring in the local cops. They'd have too many questions he couldn't or wouldn't answer. Everything was on a "need to know" basis and the locals didn't need to comprehend the situation. If they started digging into things, they'd make his job more difficult. The crooks would go underground if they realized the police wanted them.

"I can't sleep. I'm more exhausted than I've ever been in my life, but I can't doze off." Kelly interrupted his thoughts. "When I close my eyes, I see the ransacked room and I tense."

He looked away from the screen to the back seat. Their eyes met.

"I'm afraid, more scared than I've ever been. Hold me," she whispered.

Surprised by her request, he stared at her. Was that longing in her eyes or just a projection of his desire?

"Please. I feel so lost."

He got into the backseat and put his arm around her, pulling her close. She came willingly, her body trembling. The vanilla scent of her shampoo wafted to him, so delicate, so enticing. Despite that, she was trouble, a career killer, not to mention the sister of his ex-fiancé. What would Carrie think if she heard he wanted to sleep with her kid sister?

He couldn't deny a yearning for Kelly. It'd be breaking his own self-imposed rules to never again get involved with anyone from the Shaw family or with anyone he was protecting. Taking Kelly would break both rules.

She leaned against him. He felt the full appeal of her body and allowed himself the pleasure of watching her. Barely hidden by her white tank top, her budding breasts strained against the cotton fabric of her shirt. They rose and fell in synchronous movement with her breathing. Against his will, he admired her full mouth as she slept. A strand of her golden hair fell across her face. He reached to push it back behind her ear and his arm brushed against her breast.

A bolt of heat seared him and blood rushed to his groin. The need to kiss her flared. He didn't. A kiss wouldn't be enough. It would only ignite the fire that was smoldering in him. Acting on his craving couldn't do either of them any good, because it didn't solve their current problems or fix the past. It'd only make their complicated relationship more complex.

She snuggled closer and his body pulsed. Alluring, vulnerable, he could take her. She wouldn't deny him. Still, it'd be a betrayal of her trust and he'd known the sting of a friend's treachery. He wouldn't betray Kelly.

He forced his gaze away from her and back to the movie screen.

Brick woke with a start. In the dawn's light, the credits of a film were rolling on the immense movie screen. Kelly slept in his arms. Conflicting feelings stirred in him. He should have said no when she asked him to hold her. Somehow, he hadn't been able to resist her request. He closed his eyes and inhaled her scent.

She woke and stretched. "Hi," she said, her voice husky with sleep.

Hell. Why did she have to be so damn beautiful in the morning?

He ignored his growing need for her. "Morning. Let's find a restaurant and get some coffee and something to eat."

"Sounds good." She adjusted her tank top.

He pretended not to notice.

Chapter 11

Reno is a twenty-four-hour town and even at five-thirty in the morning it didn't take long to find an open coffee shop.

While Kelly freshened up in the bathroom, Brick took a seat at a table in the back corner of the room.

A bone-thin, middle-aged waitress dressed in an orange uniform with a white apron served coffee and gave him a menu. Without looking at the menu, he ordered bacon, eggs, and toast.

He rummaged through the plastic bag that held Amanda's trash, annoyed she was his only lead. The wastebasket's contents held crumpled binder paper, candy wrappers, and empty cigarette packs, but little information. The only thing he found that might help was a flyer from a local nightclub. He read the bold fonts; a special Goth Industrial show was on tonight. Doors opened at eleven-thirty pm.

With the flyer stored in his pocket, he knotted the plastic bag and put it under the table. Tonight, he'd see if Amanda showed up. Clubs weren't in full swing until after midnight. It looked like it was going to be another long night.

Shattered Rules

Kelly returned and sat in a chair across the table from him. "Toast and coffee please," she said when the waitress returned to the table.

"What did you find in her trash?"

"She eats too much chocolate. The bag is filled with candy wrappers and this." He slid the flyer toward her. "It looks like we're in for a Gothic show tonight."

She read the notice.

He took a sip of coffee and looked out of the cafe's window. The street was virtually empty at this time of the morning. Sitting back, he drank more of the insipid liquid. It did nothing to rev his engine. He'd need to drink at least three or four cups of this brown water to get the caffeine needed to manage the day and the long night ahead.

***

At eleven p.m. they stood in line waiting to enter the Goth nightclub. It was in a rundown building located in an alley in the older part of Reno. No marquee hung on the building. The flyer, they'd seen, was taped to a plain door.

A tall man in a black tux wearing skull and cross-bone earrings stood at the entrance. He asked for a ten-dollar per person cover charge. Brick paid. Kelly made a mental note to pay him back, along with the cost of the wig he bought.

"When we go in, you look for Amanda. I'll take a seat where I can see most of the dance floor. Signal me, if you need me," he whispered in her ear.

She nodded and tried to shake the creepy feeling that snaked down her spine.

Two giant stone gargoyles, sitting on faux black marble columns, stood guard at the entry of the club. In the grand ballroom, she let her eyes adjust to the dim light. The windowless walls were draped in black velvet from floor to ceiling. Tables and chairs were scattered around the room. Couches and an immense pool table sat in one corner of the room. A gigantic mirrored ball hung from a center rafter and flecks of light bounced off the attendees.

Early by Goth standards, the room was almost empty. Jarring music played while a few people danced in flowing movements. Some people seemed to be dancing with partners and the others were on the dance floor alone. It didn't seem to matter.

Though their hair might be red, blue, or green, stripes or checkerboard, the attire was black. How many shades of black were there?

With everyone dressed in dark clothes, Kelly was out of place with blue and white clothes and blonde hair. A few patrons glared, but most people ignored her.

As the night progressed the crowd grew larger. All the blackness became oppressive. Gothic music swelled. A sea of undulating bodies moving to the strains of the odd music surrounded her. The room set her nerves on edge and she suppressed an urge to run out to the lighted street.

Afraid of the dark, are you? She laughed.

Brick sat at one of the tables placed at the edge of the dance floor. She let out a sigh of relief when she saw him. He was watching over her.

She made her way around the room. Looking for Amanda, she eyed every woman who had maroon hair and was about to go to Brick and tell him her roommate wasn't there when a woman approached her.

It took a moment for her to realize it was Amanda. Her once maroon hair was now black with a bright blue stripe. A low-cut, floor-length black taffeta dress showcased her curvaceous figure. Long fishnet gloves adorned her, from her slender fingers to her arms, stopping at the elbows. A silver-studded dog collar surrounded her delicate neck. Her spider web and butterfly tattoo stood out on the pale skin of her upper right arm. Lips painted black and a heavy layer of black eyeliner made her look as if she were made up for Halloween even though it was still June.

"My God girl, what have you gotten yourself into?" Amanda yelled over the din of the music. "Answer me."

"What do you mean?"

"I had to leave my apartment because of you. Some creep came looking for you. He scared the hell out of me." Amanda held a drink in her hand and her words were slurred. She wobbled on her stilettos.

"I'm sorry."

"Yeah? That doesn't get my apartment back. Does it, Kell?"

"Who was he? What did he look like?"

As Amanda described him, Kelly realized it was the same man who attacked her in her home, the tall man who'd worn the signet ring.

"What kind of shit have you gotten into?

"Uh, it's a long story. I'm sorry you got involved."

"Yeah. Me too. Some guy called me and offered to pay me if I'd tell him what I know about you?"

"About me?"

"Yeah."

"Amanda, what did he want?"

"Anything about you."

"And you told him?"

"I needed money. My stinking boyfriend ran off with all my stuff. He even took my car. I have to take a frigging bus everywhere."

"You sold me out."

Amanda jumped back and spilled her drink. "Kelly, don't you see? I needed the money so I could stay in school. I don't have a family. If I can't help myself, nobody's gonna help me. I got to go." She spun around and walked away.

"Amanda, wait! Don't go." Kelly shouted over the loud music. "I'm not going to cause any trouble. I just need your help."

The roommate stopped and faced her.

"Help me, Amanda, and maybe I can do something for you."

Her roommates' eyes widened, "What?"

"I don't know. I don't have much money, but there must be something I could do."

Amanda took a sip of the drink she was holding. "Where's your hunk?"

"My what?"

"Your boyfriend."

"You mean Brick? He's over there at a table."

She glanced in the direction Kelly pointed.

"Sweet heaven, he's one big hunk of a man. Girl, if you ever want to kick him to the curb, you tell me and I'll take him off your hands."

Kelly choked, but she managed to nod.

"He looks tough enough to handle almost anything. I have a little trouble with my ex-boyfriend."

"Oh." She waited, wondering what that had to do with Brick.

"He's got my car and I want it back. It's mine. It's registered to me. The creep won't bring it back."

"What can I do?"

"I want you to have your boyfriend jack it for me."

"You mean steal it?"

"It's not stealing, the damn car's mine."

"Well, I—I" Kelly took a deep breath. She'd be asking an FBI agent to steal a car for her roommate. "I don't know if I can do that." She imagined Brick's angry reaction. She'd be crazy to think of asking him.

"Then I guess you don't care how to get a hold of the man who's been paying for information about you," Amanda interrupted her.

"Are you saying you know where to find him?"

For a moment, her roommate was silent.

"Amanda, is that what you're suggesting?"

"I'm just saying you help me and I'll help you." She smiled sweetly.

"I have to know you'll make it easier for me to get a hold of the man."

"How about his phone number?"

"You have it?"

"I'll give you his name and number."

"Is that the truth?"

"I need my car," Amanda whined. "Look girl, I really can tell you." Just then, the music rose in volume and she raised her voice. "Kelly, tell me if you're interested because after I finish my drink, I'm out of here. Gone from this damn town, and you'll never see me again."

"Okay. Okay. Come with me and I'll talk to Brick."

***

The pounding of the industrial music hammered Brick. He ran his hand over his forehead and wished he had earplugs. After being up all last night, he'd like to leave the Goth club and get a good night's sleep.

The spinning mirrored ball flashed, throwing flecks of light on the dancers. Just then he caught a glimpse of Kelly. She didn't fit into the milieu, but that made it easier for him to follow her in the crowd. She zigzagged her way through the swaying crowd, making slow progress toward him. A woman he guessed was her roommate followed close behind. They joined him at the table.

"You want me to what?" Brick's voice boomed, just as the music changed to something quiet. People sitting at the next table stared at him.

"You've got to be kidding," he said, lowering his voice. "I'm not a repo man."

"It's not stealing," Amanda said. "It's my car, and my jerk of a boyfriend took it. You got to get it back for me. You've got to."

Annoyance pricked the back of his neck. He was tempted to stop this right now. He'd take Amanda into custody and hold her as a material witness. It wouldn't be long before she gave up everything she knew. But if someone was watching her, he didn't want that person to know the FBI was involved. And if he took the roommate into custody, Kelly would be upset. She'd jump to her defense and start to question his motives. To keep a low profile, he decided to play along with the women, at least for a little longer.

"Can you prove the vehicle is yours?"

"I've got the pink slip."

"Where is it?"

"Why? I told you it's my car."

He glared.

"It's in my motel room."

"What about the phone number of the man?" Kelly asked.

"That's at the motel too." She finished her drink and burped. "You going to help me or not?"

"If you can show it's yours, we can talk."

"It's mine."

"Then let's go get the pink slip." Brick stood up from the table.

Amanda burped again, stood and swayed, but managed to walk out under her own power.

***

They all rode together in Brick's auto. The motel was only a few blocks away from the club.

A blast of wind sent litter swirling on the dirty street. The motel was in the kind of neighborhood Brick wouldn't want any woman to be in alone. In his career, he'd spent too many hours undercover in neighborhoods like this one. The hair on the back of his neck prickled and he wished he hadn't brought Kelly with him.

The street light near the motel was burnt out and the night seemed darker than it had on the main thoroughfare. After one a.m., the road was quiet enough. An old man huddled in a doorway of one of the rundown buildings next to the motel and two shabbily dressed men sat on the curb sharing a bottle, a nightcap, before the oblivion of a wine-soaked sleep overtook them.

Brick steered the Volvo around the men and into the pothole-infested motel parking lot. The building had probably once been white, but now it was just dingy. On the roof, a cobalt blue neon sign flashed the word "Motel." Apparently, no one had cared enough to name the motor inn. A static red neon sign proclaimed a vacancy. No surprise there.

Amanda pointed to her room and he parked in the space in front of the door.

She and Kelly went to the room to locate the pink slip.

***

The man in the nearby doorway watched the sedan enter the motel parking lot and park. Two women got out and went into a room. "Bingo." He smiled. Amanda was back and she had Kelly with her. The little bitch did know where to find her.

He scratched his hand and dug his fingernail into the rash near his signet ring. *Shit.* He'd paid the roommate while she told him lies. However, without realizing it, she had led him to Kelly. He rubbed his hands together. After he took care of Kelly, he'd come back and fix Amanda. Nobody lied to him, took his money, and got away with it. He walked to the rental truck parked nearby and waited.

Chapter 12

After Kelly and Amanda left the car, Brick unlocked the glove compartment and took out his holstered nine-millimeter handgun. He strapped it on and covered it by pulling on his black windbreaker.

The minutes passed. Impatient, he grunted. The car window was open and the smell of urine turned his stomach. He wanted Kelly out of this neighborhood, pronto.

They needed the information. Still, if Amanda thought he was going to commit grand theft auto for her, she could think again. He'd give her a couple hundred dollars if she came back with the phone number. That was more than she deserved.

When the women returned to the car. Amanda carried a shopping bag. "I've got scads of paper." She shoved her hand into the paper bag. "I had to leave my apartment so fast I just dumped it all into this damn shopping bag, but I know the pink slip is in here."

Homework notes and receipts were scattered all over the backseat. Amanda read each note she found. Kelly helped.

Brick squelched an expletive and tried to be patient. He glanced out of the car window and searched the parking lot for movement. The two people who sat at the curb were still there, but the man who'd been in the doorway was gone.

"I got it." A triumphant smile spread across Amanda's face. She handed the proof of ownership to him. "This shows I own the car."

"It looks okay. The car seems to be yours." He handed it back to her.

"Then you're going to grab my car for me?"

"I just can't go stealing autos. See a lawyer. I'll give you the name of a good attorney and a couple of hundred bucks to get you started."

"But you said…"

"I said we could talk. Do you want the two hundred?"

"Yeah, but that's not going to get my car back." Amanda's eyes filled with tears.

He wondered if they were real tears or crocodile tears. Maybe she could cry anytime she didn't get what she wanted. Nonetheless, tears spilled out of her eyes washing black eyeliner down her cheeks.

He glanced at Kelly and saw her expression soften. She was feeling sorry for her roommate. The faster he got her away from Amanda the better.

A car raced into the parking lot. The sub-compact flew over the speed bumps and screeched into an empty parking space a few yards away.

A man, the size of a linebacker, jumped out of the car. Dressed in shorts and a tank top, his muscle-bound body flexed. He ran his huge hand over his shaved head as he scrutinized the area.

"That's Norm, my boyfriend. I knew the jerk would stay here. He's driving my car." Amanda threw open the sedan's back door and ran toward the guy.

She stopped a few feet away from her vehicle. "Hey creep, give me my car."

"Who's going to make me? You bitch? You going to make me?"

"Yeah. I've got my pink slip." She waved it at him. "And I'm hiring a lawyer."

"Give me that." Norm held his beefy hand out to her. "Give me my car."

Brick watched her hide the pink slip behind her back.

"Hell," Brick whispered. He didn't want to get involved in a domestic dispute. It wouldn't help Kelly or the FBI. Still, it looked as if Amanda was determined to fight with her bodybuilder friend.

If anything happened to her, they'd never get the name of the man who wanted information on Kelly.

"Kelly, stay in the car. I'll be right back." Brick ran toward the couple.

"Hand it over," the boyfriend demanded.

In a flash, Norm rushed to her and twisted her arm, but Amanda held the pink slip. He slapped her, knocking her to the ground. She shrieked. He picked her up by her neck, choking off her cry. Amazingly, she held on to the paper.

Brick moved closer. "Let her go." The boyfriend's eyes darted from Amanda to him. Brick noticed perspiration bead up on the man's forehead.

The Volvo door opened and closed. Kelly was out of the car. In his peripheral vision, he saw her edge toward them.

The jerk still had his hands around his girlfriend's neck. He could snap it in an instant.

"It's okay buddy. Don't hurt her. I'm not going to do anything. She's your woman. You don't want to harm her."

He watched Amanda's face turn a pale shade of blue as Norm squeezed her.

101

"Let go now!"

Norm relaxed his hold and some pink came back to her face.

"Who are you, asshole?" Norm's face flushed red and his free hand flexed into a fist.

"I'm the asshole who wants you to let your lady go. Release her now and we can all go home."

"It's not your business, asshole."

Brick's back muscles tensed. The girl was in danger of dying from a broken neck.

"I'm willing to listen to your side, but first release her. Then we'll go have a beer."

"You get out of here before I break her in two!" Norm hissed.

The longer this went on the more likely Amanda would end up dead. "If you don't let her go, I am going to have to take you in."

"You some kind of cop?"

"Yeah, I'm some kind of cop."

Just then, Amanda moaned and tried again to free herself from her boyfriend's grip. The pink slip she'd been holding, dropped from her hand.

Kelly ran to pick it up.

Still clutching Amanda, Norm swung at Kelly with his free hand.

She gasped and air whooshed from her lungs as she dropped to the ground. The pink slip floated to the ground next to her.

Stunned, Brick watched Kelly lying lifeless on the ground. Before he could go to her, the boyfriend threw Amanda to the ground and, with a grunt, charged him.

Instead of trying to stop over two hundred pounds of raging power, he used Norm's momentum against him. He yanked the man forward and sent the boyfriend

102

sprawling face down on the blacktop. With his knee on the man's back, Brick put his considerable weight on the man.

"Get off me, asshole!"

"Put your hands behind you."

Brick applied more pressure on the man. "Hands behind your back."

The guy complied and he secured the man with the handcuffs he had in his jacket pocket.

"Norm, look at me." Brick yanked the guy's shoulder.

The guy lifted his face off the blacktop and twisted his head to glare at him.

"Try anything and I'll make sure you regret it." He allowed his holstered gun to be seen under the windbreaker he wore. Norm's eyes widened as he stared at the weapon, but he said nothing.

There was a rustle of taffeta as Amanda got up. "He tore my clothes, my beautiful." She coughed. "My beautiful dress." She patted her outfit as if it were an animal. "You jerk." She coughed again and cleared her throat.

Brick glanced at Kelly lying motionless on the ground. He didn't dare go to her until he'd rendered the boyfriend harmless. He looked for a place to put him.

Kelly's roommate ran toward her motel room and returned carrying her suitcase. She stopped long enough to retrieve the pink slip that lay near Kelly's still body.

"What about the phone number you promised to give us?" Brick shouted.

She threw a wadded piece of paper in his direction. Then, without so much as checking on Kelly or a thank you, she jumped into her sedan and drove away.

Norm lifted his head off the pavement and yelled, "Bitch!"

"What did you say?" Brick glared at him.

"Nothing."

"Keep it that way."

Brick glanced at Kelly again and prayed she was all right. Her eyes were open, but she wasn't moving.

Near the motel's office, he spied a metal flagpole, secured to the ground with concrete. "Stand up and move to the pole."

The guy looked at it and then at the bulge the gun made under Brick's coat and nodded.

"Put your arms around the pole." He fixed the boyfriend's wrists together with a zip tie and released the handcuffs, placing them back in his jacket pocket. The jerk wasn't going anywhere until the FBI picked him up and took him into custody.

He knelt next to Kelly and she stared at him with clear eyes. A strange wheeze came from her throat when she tried to speak.

"Don't talk. Just nod. Does anything hurt?"

She shook her head.

"Try and take a breath—did that hurt?"

"No." Her voice cracked.

"Good. I'm going to help you sit up. Take it slow."

"That hurts," she whispered.

"I think you're going to have one heck of a bruise where he hit you," he said. "But I don't think anything is broken. He must have knocked the air out of you. Can you get up?"

She nodded.

He helped her walk to the car and sit in the passenger seat.

"We'll leave for the cabin after the FBI gets here. The Bureau can hold Norm as a material witness until I can find out how he fits into this mess. Are you sure you're okay?"

"Yeah," she said in a weak voice. "I just want to go back to my cabin."

***

Forty-five minutes later, Brick parked in the cabin's garage.

"I'm so cold," Kelly said when they entered the house.

"You need rest. Why don't you go to bed, Kelly? I'll bring you a hot cup of tea."

"Thanks."

In the kitchen he rummaged through the cupboards looking for tea, hoping there was some. What did he understand about making the drink? Hot water and a bag, right?

He'd been crazy to take Kelly into that situation? He'd led her into a situation where she could've been seriously injured. Dealing with a domestic dispute was never easy, never clean. He shouldn't have let her be involved in that predicament.

Too many times he'd seen an innocent bystander hurt. His charge, Annie, had taught him how horribly wrong things could go. She'd been his responsibility and she'd died. He swallowed the bitter memory and rebuked himself. Now that he'd made it his job to protect Kelly, he needed to be sure she was kept out of the line of fire. He'd damn well do it right this time.

He put two steaming cups of tea on a tray and walked to the bedroom.

The only light in the bedroom came from the gas fireplace, giving everything an orange hue. Propped up by two king-sized pillows, Kelly sat in the middle of the huge four-poster bed. Her hair spread out on the pillow and glistened gold in the fire's light. With a warm smile, she gazed at him, an expression of trust on her face. He couldn't look her in the eye. He was using her in a game she knew nothing about. Once again, guilt slashed him.

When he handed her the cup of tea, his fingers brushed hers and static electricity sent a shock through him. He watched her delicate pink tongue catch a drip of golden liquid that ran down the teacup.

"Good," she said, licking her lips and smiling.

Heat stirred in him and he hadn't tasted the hot tea.

"You must be cold. Come under the covers." She threw back the comforter and patted the bed next to her. "Sit with me."

He wasn't cold. He was about to ignite. He examined the room, there was no chair.

"Uh, not a good idea."

She frowned.

"But too tempting to resist." He slipped off his shoes. sat on the bed, and leaned back against the headboard, careful their bodies didn't touch. Nonetheless, her warmth singed him. He took a sip of the hot tea, wishing it were ice water.

The flames in the fireplace danced.

She handed him her half-empty teacup and he put it on the nightstand next to his empty one.

"Brick."

"What is it?" He finally faced her.

"Nothing. Just Brick. I like to say it. It feels so good on my tongue," she said breathlessly.

"Brick." Her full luscious mouth made almost no sound as she formed his name.

Reaching out, he touched her cheek with his fingertips, a light caress. His eyes locked with hers. With lips parted and her eyes closed, she sighed when his lips met hers.

Shattered Rules

Her soft body pressed hard against him. A jolt of fire shot through him, but he kept his kiss gentle. Carefully, he eased his tongue into her lush, honeyed mouth and she opened wide to accept him, a soft moan answering his request for more.

Her tongue flirted with his. Chills went through him. Her fingers combed his hair and then moved down his back. He pulled her closer. This was what he'd wanted since he'd seen her in bed at the motel.

She tilted her head back and he laid kisses on her slim neck. Through the cotton fabric of her shirt, he caressed the tightened bud of her breast. She moaned his name, increasing his desire. He touched her again. Then he demanded more from her kiss. His hands explored her contours. Her breathing quickened as her body moved rhythmically with his.

Ignoring his desire for more, he pulled his mouth from hers. Her longing for him was just a symptom of her need to feel safe, a want born out of fear.

"Kelly, I have to go."

Chapter 13

"I can't stay with you."

"Why?" Kelly frowned.

"It wouldn't be right. You're hurt." Brick stood up from the bed.

"But I need you."

He saw the truth of that statement in her budded breasts, rapid breathing, and the longing that blazed in her eyes. He gently touched her lips and she licked his fingertips.

His need for her was a painful ache. Damn the FBI for putting him in this situation. It ignited a hunger for her.

"Please, don't go."

"I have to."

"Why."

"Because more than anything else in the world, I want to stay."

A look of confusion spread across her lovely face. "I don't get it."

"I know."

She couldn't understand the guilt he felt for using her or realize the pressure the FBI put him under to find out something and report back as soon as possible. If he touched her, he'd lose his creditability and end his career with the Bureau. And he didn't want to hurt Kelly. She'd eventually find out he'd used her to obtain information on Johnny Vega. Still, she wouldn't be able to say he had taken sexual advantage of her.

With all the willpower he could muster, he walked out of her room. He was able to leave Kelly because he was sure he was doing the right thing for both of them.

He'd promised to protect her. He just hadn't realized how hard it'd be to defend her from him.

The bedroom door closed quietly behind him.

Brick's exhaustion grew with each step. He climbed the stairs and took the first bedroom he found. Decorated in whitewashed pine furniture, it was a pleasant room, but the main attraction for him was the king-sized bed. It was long enough to accommodate his lengthy body. How many nights had it been since he slept in a bed? Too many.

The cell phone battery was dead. He plugged it into its charger and then found bedding in a cupboard. After quickly making the bed, he stripped down to his boxers and extinguished the light. Unable to sleep, he lay in the dark and listened to the silence.

After the betrayals of the last few years, he'd guarded his emotions, keeping them so sheltered from view, that even he wasn't sure what he felt. But sitting in the bed next to Kelly, raw feelings threatened to erupt. She'd almost disarmed him and caused him to discard the protective shell he'd built around himself.

He'd bared his soul to Kelly's sister, Carrie. He'd shared his dreams with her and the consequences had been dismissal and excruciating emotional pain. Since then, he'd made sure no one got too close. His rules: no close relationships, no ties, no love.

Kelly tempted him. There wouldn't be any point denying he wanted her. He did. But her sister had taught him a bitter lesson. And Kelly and Carrie were made from the same cloth. The same DNA ran in their veins. Only a fool would open up to pain and anguish twice. He was no fool. The saying "Once burned twice shy" held meaning for him.

A vision of Kelly, her passionate expression and luscious lips nearly undid him. He craved her with a desire stronger than any he had ever experienced for any woman, even Carrie.

He sat up in bed. His body poised and ready to give, he could fill her and satisfy his craving. She was probably still awake and she had asked for it. He stopped the thought and laid back down. There were more important things to think about.

He remembered his boss telling him that the Sierra Nevada snowpack had melted into the Truckee River and a dead FBI agent, Jack Anson, was found floating face down in the icy water. The memory hit him like a cold shower. It put life into perspective. His petty desires and infatuations were unimportant.

An hour later, without turning on a light, he slipped on his clothes and pulled on his holstered gun. With a pillow and comforter tucked under his arm, he went downstairs and stretched out on the sofa in the great room, a better place to guard Kelly.

When he finally slept, Annie's face came into focus. Stress pricked his scalp and tensed his spine. He knew what was coming and tried to wake up but couldn't. As if someone had already pressed the play button for a movie, a familiar nightmare began to run.

It was just as it had happened years earlier. Guarding Annie, a government witness about to testify in court, he entered the large federal courthouse with her. Walking next to her, their footsteps echoed on the marble floor of the huge rotunda.

Suddenly, Annie's terrified screams gripped his attention. Then he felt body-racking pain as a bullet hit his right knee and then the burn of a bullet as it grazed his right temple.

As he dropped to the floor, he saw Annie take a bullet in the chest. Bloodred splatter made a wide pattern on her white blouse.

"No!" he shouted.

Shock and disbelief shone on her young face. She collapsed.

Betrayed by his FBI partner's greed, they had been caught in an ambush. He lay wounded on the floor of the courthouse, his right knee twisted grotesquely behind him. Unable to move toward her, he stared at Annie. She lay just out of reach, their blood commingling on the cold Carrara marble floor.

Incapable of speaking, she beseeched him with her green eyes. Begging for his help, a blood-stained hand stretched out to him.

Blood dripped from his head wound into his eyes. He wiped it away and tried once more to crawl toward her. No good. Retching in pain, he watched in horror as her beautiful young face grew pale. Each beat of her heart squeezed her life's fluid from the gaping chest wound. It dripped to the floor in rhythm with her breathing. Her terrified eyes pleaded for his help until finally, her life ended. Vacant eyes stared at him, blaming him for her untimely death.

From the searing pain of a bullet and the agonizing pain of failure, useless anger whelmed up inside of him. He fought to wake up.

Awake and covered with sweat, he lived with the bitter memory. As Annie's bodyguard, he should've saved her or at least comforted her, but he hadn't. She was dead and he was alive. No bodyguard should ever let that happen. He should've kept her alive or died trying.

He swallowed to push back the stomach acid burning his throat. He squinted, then squeezed his eyes closed. He had to obliterate Annie's dead face from his vision. With his hand on his perspiration-covered forehead, he forced his eyes open again and stared into the dark.

After almost five years, he'd learned to live with his failure and guilt. He couldn't live with it if anything happened to Kelly. With a groan, he felt the familiar heaviness in his chest. One death on his conscience was all he could take.

***

Kelly lay awake for hours wondering if she was angry at Brick or grateful to him. He was right, of course, not to respond to her. Her cheeks burned with embarrassment. She'd let her body's desire override her good sense. That hadn't happened before. She'd make sure it never did again.

When she was with Johnny, she'd never wanted him the way she desired Brick. It stunned her to realize she'd only dated Johnny out of ignorance and a wish to rebel against her sister's strict rules. If she were honest, she'd admit that since she was a teenager, she hadn't stopped caring for the one man she couldn't have—Brick.

This wasn't the time to complicate her life with an affair with her sister's ex-fiancé. It could only lead to hurt and she'd had enough. Still, a sense of longing for him shook her.

Shattered Rules

With an uncertain future, she wanted Brick to be concerned that soon she might be dead, gone from the earth almost as if she had never existed.

If the intruders had their way, she'd be murdered with few people to note her demise or feel the void left by her passing. Tears pushed against her eyelids, but she wouldn't cry. With so few days left to live, she wouldn't waste time shedding tears. Nonetheless, one fleeing tear managed to slide down her cheek. She quickly wiped it away. She hadn't told Brick the whole truth. She didn't deserve his concern.

Her lips were still swollen from his kiss. The taste of him lingered. Her body heated. She wanted him. No. She corrected that thought. She wanted to share a love with him, spend a lifetime with him, an impossible dream. With a moan, she lay back against the pillows and closed her eyes.

Somehow, she'd survive. She hadn't yet left a big enough footprint on the sands of time. Even if she didn't deserve Brick's love, it was too early to die.

***

The intruder could see Kelly's cabin through the brush on the empty lot. In the cab of a parked pick-up truck, the man watched for movement in the house. He zipped his padded jacket. "Another damned cold night," he swore under his breath and tucked a blanket around his legs and checked his holstered nine-millimeter weapon. "I'm damned tired of sitting around watching these people." If something didn't occur shortly, he'd make it happen. He let his shoulders relax and smiled at the thought of killing again.

***

Brick woke from his restless sleep. He could get up and make a pot of coffee or allow himself the luxury of more rest. Still bone tired, he turned away from the light coming from the windows in the great room and closed his eyes. It crossed his mind he was avoiding the time when he'd have to see Kelly. He didn't examine the thought.

At nine o'clock, he couldn't sleep any longer. Before making his way to the kitchen, he stopped outside her bedroom and peeked in. Angelic, she lay asleep and exposed in her tank top and underpants. As he scanned her, he listened to her rhythmic breathing. What would it be like to lie down next to her and run his hand down her soft form? Cursing his desire for her, he quietly closed the door.

In the kitchen, he found the Italian roast coffee beans, made a pot of coffee, and took a full mug out to the back deck overlooking the lapping water of Lake Tahoe. In a teak deck chair facing the turquoise water, he sipped the thick liquid and counted the days until this assignment was over.

After he was shot, he'd turned down a chance to resign with benefits. He'd never quit. The FBI was his life. It was all he had, all he wanted. If it hadn't been for Don asking him to check on Kelly, he'd be in his new office in San Francisco orienting himself to his assignments there.

When this mission was over, he wouldn't see her again. Before he'd started this job, his mind had been filled with thoughts of a new start in San Francisco. Now it was hard to concentrate on anything but Kelly.

A gust of wind rustled the leaves of the birch trees at the water's edge, a sound so gentle it wouldn't be heard above the traffic noise in San Francisco's South Bay. Maybe he needed the city noise to keep his mind filled so he couldn't hear the sound of his lost dream of a wife and kids.

Here in the Sierra Nevada mountain range, it was hard to ignore the longing pounding in his chest. *Enough.*

He checked on Amanda's boyfriend, Norman Rampac, and was told he was a local bad boy. Recently accused of petty theft and taking drugs, the man had an outstanding warrant. Reno Police would use it to hold him for now.

The scrap of paper he got from Amanda was still in his pants pocket. He retrieved it and punched in the number. It rang four times and then a voice message picked up. "Leave your name, number, and the date and time you called."

The message gave no clue as to who owned the number. It was so short it'd be difficult to recognize the voice if he heard it again. Damned waste of time, everything they'd gone through last night was for nothing. He was no closer to finding out who ransacked Kelly's house or who paid for information about her.

Out of the corner of his eye, he noticed a flash of light near the grove of trees where he had first parked his car. He picked up his mug, took a sip of coffee, and casually looked in the direction of the trees. There it was again, another flash. Was it a reflection of light off a pair of binoculars?

He walked slowly to the backdoor, careful not to look in the direction of the trees again. Opening the door to the cabin, he ran into Kelly on her way outside.

"Go back. Someone's watching the cabin." He pushed her back into the living room. "I saw something on the ridge near the grove of pines. Stay here. I'm going to take a look." He started to leave, then turned and said, "Stay here and this time I mean it. I'm going out through the side door in the garage and try to circle around the cabin to see if I can take a look at him."

"Don't go."

"I've got to. Remember, stay in the house until I come back. Keep away from the windows. I don't want whoever it is to see you."

"Okay, but Brick."

"Yeah."

"Be careful."

***

The brush near the cabin gave good cover. Brick was able to make it to the edge of the property without being seen.

A man with black hair, black jeans, and a black T-shirt crouched next to a pine tree, his expression grim. He didn't look at the wonders of the Sierra Mountains or Lake Tahoe. Staring toward the Shaw cabin, he held high-powered binoculars to his eyes.

From his angle, Brick couldn't see a weapon, but he couldn't be sure the man didn't have one. The guy put down his binoculars and stood, appearing to be making a decision. Wiping his hands on his jeans, he picked up the binoculars again and peered at the cabin.

Brick gazed in that direction as well. He hoped Kelly had done as she was told and stayed the hell away from the windows. He turned back in the direction of the stranger.

Just then their eyes met. The man's brown eyes widened and he ran.

"Wait!" Slipping and sliding, Brick found it difficult to get traction on the floor of pine needles.

The man paused to pick up his binocular case and Brick tackled the guy. They rolled on the ground and he felt every chunk of Sierra Nevada granite that lay under the carpet of pine needles.

The athletic stranger punched him, and then used the high-powered binoculars as a weapon, beating him about the head.

His skin broke open above his eye. Warm blood ran down his face. Now he was pissed. He ducked from another punch and sent a blow to the man's midsection, then hit him again for good measure. The stranger dropped to the ground. He forced the man's hands behind his back and secured them with his handcuffs. *Damn.* He sure didn't think he'd have to use the cuffs again so soon.

"What the hell!" the man yelled.

"Shut up." He reached into his pocket, pulled out his FBI identification, and put it in the guy's face.

The man froze.

"Why were you watching the house?" He shoved his ID back in his pocket.

"I didn't break any laws."

"Why are you here?"

"I don't have to tell you."

"Answer my question or I'm taking your ass to the FBI office. You can answer questions there."

"I got nothing to say."

"About what?"

"About anything."

"Most people watch the lake. Why were you watching that house?"

The sun beat down on Brick and a wasp buzzed his head. He swatted it away and waited for an answer. A trickle of blood ran down his neck. He reached up and felt a cut on his ear where the binoculars had hit him.

Reggi Allder

"If I don't get a straight answer, I'm arresting your sorry ass and holding you until you have something to say or until you're old enough to be a grandfather."

No response.

"I'll give you an easy question."

"What's your name?"

No answer.

"Okay buddy, get up."

"James."

"James what?"

"Just James."

"Why are you here?"

"I'm not telling you anything else."

"Okay, buddy. You're on the way to jail." He yanked the guy to a standing position and pushed him forward.

As they approached the needle-covered trail, the guy jabbed him in the ribs and tried to run. He grabbed the guy. They lost their footing and tumbled down a steep slope.

Chapter 14

Brick rolled down the embankment until his right knee hit a granite boulder. A jolt of pain shot through him, but the rock stopped his descent.

James fell a few yards further down the slope, before coming to a stop in the mud of a minor creek that meandered toward Lake Tahoe.

Ignoring the burning sensation in his leg, he jumped up and limped to where James lay on his back.

"Get up."

"I can't. My hands are still cuffed."

He yanked the man to a standing position. "Try something else and I'll make sure you do time. Now walk or I'll drag you to the cabin."

The man glared at him but moved toward the cabin.

In order not to startle Kelly and remind her of the attack at her home in Palo Alto, he called her name. Then he entered the living room, with his quarry in tow.

"Sit down. Over there on the hearth."

James sat.

"If you cooperate, I'll remove the cuffs."

There was that look again, the angry eyes of a trapped animal.

Kelly entered the living room and stared. "Brick, what happened?"

"Jamie is that you? What's going on? Why are you handcuffed?"

"This guy was spying on the cabin with binoculars."

She turned her back on him and smiled at James. "You weren't spying, were you, Jamie?"

He shrugged and looked down as if to admire the old carpet.

"I'll get you a cup of coffee or would you rather have a glass of water?"

She treated the man as if he had dropped by for a neighborly chat. She didn't realize it, but she was playing good cop to his bad cop, a well-known interrogation technique.

"Water would be good?" James smiled.

"I'll be right back."

Brick ran a hand over his jaw. His ear throbbed and he was developing one hell of a headache. He reached up and felt a bump forming on the side of his head. He must have hit it when he rolled down the embankment or was it a hit from the binoculars?

Jamie's feral eyes tracked his every move.

Kelly re-entered the living room carrying a tray with a pitcher of ice water and one glass tumbler. It seemed he wasn't being offered anything to quench his thirst, punishment no doubt for a perceived mistreatment of her friend, Jamie.

She set the tray on the coffee table in front of the sofa and glared at him with narrowed eyes.

"Undo the man's hands, Brick. How can he drink the water? Jamie, you won't do anything foolish, will you?"

He shook his head, but his body was tense and an angry expression pulled on his taut features.

120

Shattered Rules

Holding the key to the cuffs, Brick leaned over the man and whispered in his ear. "Make a move to hurt Kelly and it will be last the move you ever make."

He released the cuffs and put them in his pocket, then causally leaned against the living room wall, but his eyes never left James.

"More water?" Kelly asked.

"No." The man pushed his straight black hair out of his eyes, leaving a trail of mud on his forehead.

She took his glass and put it back on the tray. Then she sat in the blue velvet wing chair facing the fireplace.

For a moment, no one spoke, tension straining the atmosphere.

"Why are you here?" Brick's voice seemed to boom in the stillness.

"To warn Kelly." He ran his hands through his unruly hair.

"What could you possibly warn me about?"

"Does he have to know?" He stared at Brick.

"He's a friend, just like you."

"Kelly, he's an FBI agent."

"I know."

"Damn," Jamie took a deep breath.

Brick didn't say anything. Let the two of them work out who he was. It didn't matter to him what either of them thought as long as he got the information he wanted.

"Kelly, you know I work in room service at The Big Top."

"Yeah."

"I was in Johnny Vega's suite picking up food trays after one of his parties when I overheard him talking.

He didn't know I was still there." He exhaled slowly and rubbed his hands together as if jittery.

Brick saw Kelly's impatient expression, but she didn't interrupt him.

"Johnny was pissed as hell. He told his men to snatch you and haul you back to him. Johnny said, 'I could kill that ho. She stole my system and I don't care what you have to do, you bring that little bitch to me!'"

James swallowed hard. "When I heard that, I just got out of there."

"Oh God," Kelly whispered.

"Did you overhear anything else?" Brick asked.

"No. I just left as fast as I could and I'm not going back." He took a quick breath. "Can I have more water?"

"Sure."

She filled his glass and then Brick watched her walk up and down the living room in a random pattern going nowhere.

James finished the water and stood. "I want to go."

"You're going to be held as a material witness. You're lucky because I'm putting you in custody. That will keep you alive."

"The hell—" James twitched. "I didn't do anything."

"It's about keeping you breathing." Brick stood away from the wall he'd been leaning against and came closer to James. "You're Kelly's friend. You admit it. Johnny wants to kick her ass. You're in the way. Hence, your ass is trash. I'm offering you a way to stay alive. I'd take it."

The guy's shoulders slumped. "Shit." He looked up and, for the first time, fear shone in his widened eyes. "What did I get myself into?"

An hour later, a cab pulled up to the cabin's front door. The cabbie got out and rang the doorbell. Brick answered. An FBI agent he had worked with in LA and, who had recently transferred north, stood at the door.

"Hey, Mike, how's it going?" He shook the man's hand at the door.

"Can't complain. Got my package?"

"Yeah. I've arranged for him to be delivered to the FBI's San Francisco office. You okay with that?"

"No problem. It's a nice day for a drive." Mike smiled.

Brick didn't speak of his concern that someone in the Bureau had turned to the dark side. However, he watched the taxi speed away and hoped they'd be fine.

His back crawled as if someone was still watching him. He scanned the area and saw nothing out of the ordinary. He rubbed his temples and shook off the feeling. It was only a residual concern from earlier in the day.

In the kitchen, the throb of his head and the growl of his stomach fought for attention. His stomach won. He rummaged through the cabinets looking for food. Kelly joined him and sat at the table.

He glanced up from the cupboard and peered into her bleak eyes. "You knew Johnny was after you."

She nodded. "I couldn't stand his cruelty anymore. I told him it was over. I was leaving him. He wouldn't let me go. I was terrified of him. I waited until he trusted me again and went on a business trip. I took a chance and ran."

She paused. "He said I belonged to him. That's how he thinks of people. He owns them." She frowned. "He'll do whatever it takes to get me back. If he can't, he'll kill me."

Her statement was so simple and clear and her fear was almost palpable.

"Is there something else you're not telling me?"

"What else could there be?"

What better way for her not to answer the question than to ask another question? "There is nothing else you need to tell me, Kelly?"

"What can I say?"

Another question. He'd been sympathetic. Now, she was beginning to annoy him. He watched her squirm under his gaze. She was hiding something.

"I was an immature kid when I met Johnny. I grew up when I saw what a brute he is." She swallowed hard and blinked back a tear.

A pang of guilt rocked Brick. She thought he was protecting her. Again, he was reminded he was using her to get to Vega.

"Is there something you want to tell me?"

"What could I?" She looked away from him.

She was a terrible liar. An experienced one could've looked straight at him, with their eyes wide open and unflinching. Still, it seemed more and more like Kelly was up to her pretty little neck in some dirty business.

He pushed back the memory of the sweet, naive teenager she'd once been. The most likely scenario was that he'd eventually be forced to arrest her.

An FBI agent had been murdered. Johnny Vega was somehow involved. He now believed Kelly was too, but how? He faced her and she glanced at him with a plea for understanding in her expression.

He didn't speak. She didn't move. Silence filled the room.

A drip of blood ran down his neck. He brushed it away.

"You're bleeding!"

He reached up and felt blood oozing from the cut on his ear.

"Come into the bathroom. I'll bandage it."

"I'm fine."

"It'll only take a minute. It could get infected."

"Forget it."

"Please."

It was obvious she wasn't going to let it go until she gave him first aid. Reluctantly, he walked into the bathroom.

"You're so tall. Sit down, so I can clean the cut."

He sat on the edge of the tub. She came close to inspect the wound. Her slim leg brushed his thigh and her soft breast touched his shoulder as she leaned toward him.

Damn, his treacherous body. Her closeness sent a shard of desire through him, more painful than the cut on his ear.

"Oh God, there's blood all down your neck!"

He felt her fingers tremble as she cleaned the area with a cotton ball and peroxide.

"It's still bleeding. You need stitches."

"I'm fine."

"But…"

"Put a damn bandage on it."

"You need stitches."

"I can't sit here forever." His voice was harsher than he'd meant it to sound.

She bit her lip and pain registered in her expression. He hadn't wanted to hurt her feelings, but his ear throbbed, his head pounded, and his knee ached. He was frustrated at his lack of progress in getting information and he wanted to take Kelly in his arms and make passionate love to her. He never would.

"It's my fault you were hurt. I'm so sorry." She put a Band-Aid on the cut.

"It wasn't," he said, still sitting on the edge of the tub. She was too near. There it was again, her soft vanilla scent, sweet and delicate. Almost against his will, he pulled her to him and pressed his lips to hers.

Her mouth opened and his tongue entered.

Sighing, she pressed against him, as her legs wrapped around his thigh.

He shouldn't kiss her, shouldn't want her, but he felt so bad and she felt so good.

She aligned her body with his and he felt her body heat. She clung to him as he ran his hands down her back to the perfect curve of her buttocks. She trembled and her lips parted further, allowing his tongue to flirt with hers. He heard her ragged breath as his hands ranged over her body. She seemed to melt into him. He continued his exploration.

Chapter 15

If he didn't manage his urges, Kelly would understand the powerful emotions she'd awakened in him. Brick tensed. He wouldn't allow that. She'd know how much he wanted her. She was the wrong woman, in the wrong place, at the wrong time. A mobster's girl, again he understood involvement with her would end his career. He pushed her away.

Her eyes flew open. Raw desire still blazed in her wide eyes and her look of disappointment was unmistakable. He turned his back on her and walked out of the room.

In the hallway, pain throbbed in his temple. Penance, no doubt, for craving her. He rubbed his brow. The throb in his head and the growl of his stomach fought for his attention. The stomach won. He limped into the kitchen and put a cup of cold coffee into the microwave.

As he gulped the hot liquid, he rummaged through the cupboards. A can of mushroom soup and a can of tomato paste was all he found. He opened the soup and dumped it into a saucepan, added water, and waited for it to warm on the stove.

The liquid tasted like mildly flavored water. He needed a real meal; steak or chicken, French bread, and something green. The Tahoe City supermarket was only a few streets away. He didn't dare leave Kelly alone. His stomach growled again. She'd have to come with him.

"Soup?" he offered when she entered the kitchen. He didn't mention their kiss and was relieved the desire he'd seen in her expression was gone, replaced by irritation.

"James was stressed," she said, ignoring the question about soup.

"He has good reason to be. If he stays cool, he'll be fine."

"I'm worried about Carrie too. I thought she'd be here by now. Where is she?"

"Could be she has business to take care of."

"No. She should be here like we planned. Why doesn't she call?" She stared at him. "God help me, I'm beginning to think my sister is dead. The intruders found her or she'd be here by now."

He looked into her bleak eyes and wished he could give her a reason to believe everything was okay. He couldn't.

"Carrie's not dead. We'd have heard something. The police would've notified you."

That was almost true. Most bodies turned up soon after they were killed. However, there was a minority of cases where the victim wasn't discovered until months or even years after their death.

"She's working," he said. "You know what a workaholic Carrie is. You'll get a call when she takes a breather."

"If anything has happened to her, it's my fault." Kelly's eyes glistened with moisture.

He resisted the urge to comfort her.

***

In the rare atmosphere of the Lake Tahoe basin, Brick's appetite had come alive and demanded to be fed.

Even tired and bruised, he was forced to shop. He drove the Volvo toward the Tahoe City Supermarket. Kelly sat beside him. She didn't want to come along. He had insisted.

With the clear night, the lake reflected the moon's image. If circumstances had been different, he'd have parked beside the shore so they could enjoy the view, but tonight he drove without stopping. She didn't speak. He didn't either.

It was nearly closing time when he pulled into the market's parking lot. A few shoppers rushed through the doors before the store closed for the night. Tourists, purchasing goodies they probably wouldn't allow themselves to eat the rest of the year, filled their carts with junk food and booze.

Kelly didn't appear interested, so he arbitrarily bought food he liked. He filled the cart with enough supplies to feed them for three or four days. He picked two huge sirloin steaks, a whole chicken, and ground beef for burgers. He seized eggs, milk, cereal, French bread, oranges, and salad makings. On his way to the check stand, he grabbed a yogurt, Brie and Cheddar cheese, and water crackers, then took anything else that caught his eye, including chips, donuts, and coffee. He wanted a beer but all his wits to stay alert and on guard. A twelve-pack of cola would do, lots of caffeine to keep him awake.

On the way back to the cabin, Kelly's expression told him not to try making polite conversation. Again, he drove in silence.

The wind picked up, blowing away the clouds. The silver hue of the moon shimmering on the water made the lake even more beautiful. He glanced at Kelly. Her eyes were closed. He shrugged. Maybe that was best. She needed rest.

His back crawled. Someone was following them. In the rearview mirror, he couldn't see any unusual traffic. A white truck and a light green SUV drove behind them. A couple of blocks later, the two cars were still with him.

He drove to a gas station and got out. Though the car didn't need a fill-up, he pretended to put gas in the tank. He cleaned the windshield as both vehicles rolled by without slowing down. He made a mental note of each car as it passed.

After five minutes, he headed toward the cabin. The vehicles he'd seen were nowhere in sight.

Kelly continued to sleep.

***

The sound of the garage door opening woke Kelly. Home at last. That used to mean something, but now the cabin was just another lonely place. She missed Carrie and wanted to search Los Angeles for her but had no idea where to start. The business conference she'd attended was over. Her sister could be anywhere in the whole country.

Kelly strained to remain positive, but as time passed it became harder. There was nothing to do but wait for her sister to arrive at the cabin.

She watched Brick check the side door to the backyard. In the trunk, she picked up a bag of groceries.

A phone rang. Not Brick's phone, the landline in the cabin rang once, twice. Fumbling to get her keys out of her pocket, she dropped the grocery bag, ran to the backdoor, and put the key into the lock. Her grandparents' old answer machine started.

By the time she got into the kitchen, all she heard was, "The battery's going dead."

Carrie. She ran to the wall phone in the kitchen and grabbed the receiver. *Too late.*

"Damn!" She wanted to hit the phone in frustration.

Brick entered the kitchen carrying the bag of groceries she'd dropped and set it on the kitchen table. "Who was it?"

"Carrie."

Her heart beat so fast, that she could hardly speak. "She called. I thought—" She grabbed a quick breath. "I was beginning to think I'd never hear from her again. I was afraid." She tried to calm down. "I was terrified the men who attacked me had somehow found and killed her." She rested her head on his broad chest. His muscled arms closed around her, shielding her.

He cleared his throat. "What did Carrie say?"

"I didn't talk to her. I just heard her voice. I tried to get to the phone. I was too late."

He pushed the button on the answering machine and let the message play.

"Kelly, why the hell can't I go home? What have you done this time? Stay at the cabin and keep out of trouble until I get there. I'll try to be on the—damn, the battery's going dead."

"Why couldn't she have called five minutes later, when we were here?"

"Either way, her phone's battery would've gone dead," he reminded her. "The main thing is, she's on her way here."

"Then why do I feel so scared for her?"

His strong arms flexed, gently squeezing her. "Relax. Carrie is fine."

What was Brick's reaction to hearing her sister's voice after all these years? Or had he been in contact with her all along? Was that the reason he turned up on the doorstep in the middle of the night, to see Carrie?

He released her.

She shivered as cold air replaced his arms.

"I'll bring in the rest of the groceries."

She felt the void when he left the room.

Later, she helped put the supplies away, showing him where everything belonged. It felt right to be working in the kitchen together. *Almost like an old married couple.* Where did that thought come from? She'd better not forget that he'd once belonged to Carrie. Brick would always be her sister's man. They didn't talk, but worked as a team, each sensing what needed to be done. A comfortable silence descended on the room with only the aroma of good food to interrupt her thoughts. She watched him season the chicken with ground thyme, garlic, and bay leaves before putting it in the oven. She set the table and made a Greek salad, then put out water crackers, and French Brie for hors d'oeuvres.

When she and Carrie were children, they had spent summers here at the cabin. Fresh from swimming in the lake and still in their bathing suits, they'd run into the kitchen to help set the table for dinner. Then the kitchen had been hot and filled with the glorious aroma of buttermilk biscuits and freshly baked apple pie.

She could picture her grandmother standing at the stove, fanning herself with her brightly colored apron, her gray/blonde hair tied up in a bun, and beads of perspiration on her brow. How wonderfully simple those days had been. She wished life was still that clear.

"Dinner," Brick said as he carved the chicken he'd taken from the oven.

They sat at the table in the big country kitchen.

"Good to see you eat." He smiled. "I was getting worried."

"When I was a little girl, I told my mother I didn't need to eat because I lived on sunshine."

"You were powered by solar." He chuckled.

She laughed. It had been too long since she'd found anything funny.

After dinner, she entered the living room, opened the drapes, and watched the full moon mirrored on the lake. The birch trees swayed in a gentle breeze. The only sound was the rustle of the leaves on the tree branches. In the moonlight, Brick's eyes appeared to be silver blue.

She put a tea set on the coffee table, poured a cup, and handed it to him. He sniffed the tea and wrinkled his nose.

"Peppermint." She smiled. "Try it. You'll like it." She sat on the sofa next to him.

He took a sip. "Not bad." He took another sip, then put the cup on a nearby table.

A sense of pleasure she hadn't felt in many years, washed over her. "Why can't life be easy?" she asked.

"If it was, it wouldn't be life. Would it?" He smiled and then winked.

"I guess you're right."

"We all search for happiness and look for free will, but we're ruled by duty and are pawns of fate."

She heard the pain in his quiet voice. What duties hid in the shadows of his life?

"Kelly, we find contentment within the confines of our circumstances. Count your blessings."

"I count you as one of those blessings, Brick."

He cleared his throat.

They sat in silence. The tranquil night was interrupted only by the sound of feral cats fighting outside the cabin.

"It's a jungle out there," he joked.

She wanted to laugh. However, there was little humor because now she understood, in so many ways, his statement was true.

133

With her head resting against his shoulder, she inhaled his masculine fragrance. A warm sensation swept through her. She wanted this night to last. Soon he'd be gone. She'd never see him again.

"It's getting late. We better get some sleep." He sat up and stretched.

"Okay," she answered, not really wanting to sleep. It occurred to her they could share a bed tonight. Though she ached for him to hold her, kiss her, fill her, she knew he had no interest in doing so. She sighed.

"Is something wrong?"

"Everything's fine." She tried to force her lips into a smile. "Just fine."

"Then go to bed. I'll lock up the house."

"Thanks for helping with dinner."

He shrugged.

"Good night."

"Yeah." He left the room.

While she dressed for bed, she couldn't help thinking about his continued kindness. He didn't have to help. He could be home taking care of his own life, wherever that might be. Instead, he was with her, putting himself in danger. He must have some feelings for her, had to care just a little. Or why else would he stay?

In bed, she pictured him in the room above her. A shiver of yearning swept through her. With her eyes closed, she relived their kiss. Her budded breast tightened. She could feel his caress as he placed gentle but persuasive kisses on her neck. Her breath quickened. "Brick," she whispered.

Silence was her only answer.

An hour later she was still awake. No amount of wishing could alter one moment of the past. No amount of hope would transform her future. She had to stop torturing herself. *Don't think of Brick. He's never going to be yours.*

***

Brick checked the doors and windows, and then found a comfortable position on the sofa in the great room. He glanced at his watch. One in the morning, Kelly was dreaming by now. He pictured her in bed and remembered the sweet taste of her. *Damn.* Against his better judgment, he continued to think of her. He sat up and took a deep breath. *Focus on the job at hand.*

Tomorrow he'd call a company in Sacramento and ask them to install an alarm system in the cabin and Kelly's house in Palo Alto. If he gave the alarm company the right incentive—money, they'd do it immediately.

In a few days, his job would be over and he'd be forced to leave her. Every level of protection he arranged now gave him some assurance she'd be all right when he was gone.

Before he'd seen her again, he was sure he'd be indifferent to her plight. He'd been wrong. That took him by surprise. Living with her, touching her, and kissing her changed everything. He wasn't detached and soon his assignment would be over. Then she'd be guarded by agents who wouldn't care about her, like he did.

Chapter 16

The intruder drove the green SUV onto the graveled road that overlooked the cabin. He had to be careful. He'd almost been spotted earlier tonight when he followed Kelly, and her guy, home from the grocery store.

He turned off the auto's headlights and used only the light of the moon to steer the car toward the grove of pines near her home. He backed the vehicle under the trees and parked facing the house.

The lights went dark on the bottom floor, then went off on the second floor of the old place. He leaned against the seat and zipped his down jacket. The girl was in there. The stolen system must be close by. It wasn't in the cabin. He'd searched for it before she arrived. Nevertheless, she wouldn't have come to this mountain village if the flash drive wasn't nearby.

The last light was extinguished in the house; his prey had settled in for the night. He relaxed but didn't close his eyes.

*****

In the morning, Brick looked out the living room window to the ridge. A green SUV was pulling out from under the pines that overlooked the house. He could see a Nevada license plate, but it was too far away to read it. The driver's face was hidden behind a floppy-brimmed fishing hat and sunglasses. Just an early morning fisherman, he thought, but his skin crawled. The vehicle looked very much like the one he'd seen last night on the way back from the supermarket. He shook off his concerns, probably paranoia. After all, the mountains were filled with vehicles like that one. Anyway, the driver didn't appear to be watching the cabin and the vehicle was moving away from it.

In the bathroom, he showered and remembered Kelly kissing him, her breast brushing against him. His temperature surged. It wasn't merely her body that attracted him. Her kindness moved him. She wanted to help because he was hurt and for no other reason. At the sight of even a little blood, Carrie would've retreated and left him to bleed.

He remembered Carrie's face when she'd seen him lying in the hospital bed years earlier. She'd recoiled from him, revulsion in her expression. At that moment he'd hated her. Today, he didn't blame her. With a gash in his forehead and his eyes purple and swollen nearly shut, he'd been a horror show. More than that, she'd fallen in love with a strong, healthy guy. Then, before they were married, she'd come face to face with an invalid who might lose his leg. That was never part of their bargain. He'd promised to take care of her, not the other way around. That day she'd left his engagement ring on the hospital nightstand and he'd never seen her again.

After the breakup, he'd deceived himself as only a man betrayed by love can. He didn't need love. It was overrated and he wanted no part of it. When Carrie rejected him, a scab formed on his heart. Yesterday, it had been removed by Kelly's compassion.

Be careful. She's as undependable as her sister. Forget her. She's Johnny's girl and an FBI assignment, nothing more.

Shit. Sitting on his butt was giving him too much time to think about his feelings, something he'd always avoided. He had to spark some action. If he could get Johnny Vega pissed off, maybe the guy would make a mistake and he'd be there when Johnny did.

Kelly had to stay and wait for her sister. He didn't have to be with her every minute. After what happened at the hotel, he was sure she would keep a promise to remain in the cabin.

He punched in The Big Top casino phone number, asked for Mr. Vega, and arranged a meeting.

Two hours later, he entered the casino and found the elevator to the penthouse suite. A guard stood at the elevator door. He noted the holstered gun under the man's left arm. It ruined the line of his expensive designer suit.

Brick had locked his gun in the glove box, protected by the car's alarm. He'd never get in to see Johnny if he had a weapon.

"I'm Brick Larson here to see Johnny Vega." Then he put his arms out so the man could pat him down.

Afterward, the thug opened the elevator and let him enter. He pressed the button of the private elevator and the doors closed and the elevator rose smoothly toward the penthouse.

A travertine marble floor covered the entry of Johnny's domain. A stout middle-aged woman with blonde hair and black roots sat at a huge chrome and glass desk.

She looked up. "Mr. Larson?"

"Yeah."

"Come this way." She walked down a hallway and ushered him into a massive office.

A wall of windows, with city and desert views, dominated the room. Gold-framed original California landscapes hung from the tan suede-covered walls. A plush, modern geometric, rug was underfoot. Large antique bronzes flanked an ornate cherry wood, ormolu trimmed desk. The room held the pungent aroma of Cuban cigars.

Johnny Vega sat behind the desk and didn't get up when he entered.

Dressed in the business casual attire of linen and silk, GQ would be proud to exhibit, Johnny leaned back in his ergonomic desk chair, the epitome of sophisticated nonchalance.

Nonetheless, the guy's hawk-like eyes twitched. He scrutinized him head to foot and smiled a predatory smile.

"What do you want, Larson?" Vega finally stood up from his desk, standing as tall as his six feet three inches. Johnny leaned forward in the language of intimidation.

"I'm here to tell you to leave Kelly Shaw alone." Brick glared at Johnny.

Vega tensed. "You're out of date. I dumped the bitch and haven't seen her in weeks."

He cringed when he heard Kelly called a bitch. "You sent men to ransack her home and threaten her. Call off the goon squad."

"You're full of shit."

"I'm being real polite, Mr. Vega, but don't push your luck. Leave her alone or I'll have to come back in an official capacity. Neither of us wants that."

Johnny glared. "Who the hell are you?"

139

"It's on a "need to know" basis and right now, you don't need to. Just forget her or you'll wish you never found out who I am."

Vega's eyes narrowed. "I have friends in high places who'd take a dim view of that kind of talk."

"Really?"

"Yeah." Vega flexed his biceps and fisted his hands "No need for any trouble as I told you, I dumped the bitch." His mouth twisted into a smile. "Don't harass me, Larson."

The phony grin turned Brick's stomach. Still, he smiled back. "I'd never bother an important man like you, Mr. Vega. I only wanted to give you a heads-up so we're both on the same page. By the way, Kelly's a friend of mine. If I was convinced you were trying to hurt her, I'd be forced to stop you."

Silence filled the room.

"Tell her to return what she took," Johnny said, his voice as rough as coarse sandpaper.

"Stay away from her."

A man, dressed in a black silk suit and a red dress shirt, rushed into the office. With his dark hair slicked back, he looked like an ad for the young Mafia.

A counterpoint to Johnny's suave sophistication, he was a street thug in expensive clothes. A telltale bulge under the left arm of his designer jacket told of his concealed weapon.

"Sorry to bother you, boss, but they're waiting to start the meeting. Everybody's in the conference room."

"Let them wait. I have a call to make. Larson is leaving," Johnny said as he left the room.

"This way out." The young hood crooked his head toward the door and patted the gun under his left arm.

Shattered Rules

Satisfied Vega knew Kelly was under his protection, he followed the punk.

Halfway to the elevator, the double doors of a conference room stood open. Several men sat at a massive ebony conference table. Brick paused and tried to memorize their faces. Later, he'd pick them out of a mug book.

A slim Asian man in his late forties glared at him. The man's expression challenged him. Brick instinctively knew this man was important. Their eyes caught. He'd seen the guy before, but where?" He memorized the man's features and sensed the stranger was doing the same. Their eyes held until someone closed the conference room doors.

"Follow me," the thug said.

Brick rushed toward the elevator. He wanted to sketch the face of the man in the conference room before it faded from his memory.

Back in the car, he searched the glove compartment for the sketch pad he always carried. With a black Conte crayon, he began to draw the man's face.

***

A pang of guilt sent a quiver through Kelly. She'd told Brick she'd stay in the cabin. No matter how much she wanted to keep her word, she couldn't. Agent Ted Simmons was waiting for her. They'd go together to retrieve Johnny's flash drive. Once it was in Agent Simmons' hands, everything would be okay. She'd have her life back and her sister would too.

Looking for excitement, she'd unwittingly become involved with a vicious mobster. Now she could be implicated in—she still wasn't sure what. No matter, at this point it wouldn't do any good to understand. Soon she'd be out of it.

With a groan, she remembered the day Ted Simmons introduced himself as an FBI agent and asked for her help. Believing he was a weirdo trying to make an impression on her. She had laughed at him. He'd persisted and had shown her his identification. When she was convinced, he told her to watch Johnny and his friends. She should pay attention to his private conversations with others. Afterward, the grim underworld he functioned in had become clear.

Terrified, she'd wanted to run, but how could she say no to the FBI's request for her assistance? So, for the short term, she had stayed with Johnny. When an opportunity presented itself, she grabbed the flash drive and ran. She cringed at the memory.

After Brick left the cabin, she'd put a note on the foyer table, saying she'd return soon, then hoped he'd never read it because she'd be back before he saw it. He'd never realize she'd broken her promise.

Her fingers ached from squeezing the car's steering wheel. Her life and her sister's life depended on her getting the damned flash drive to Simmons. He'd told her it was safer if she didn't know what was on it. At the time she'd accepted that explanation. Now, she had the uncomfortable feeling that she was being used by the FBI without concern for her or her sister's safety.

Traffic was light. She'd meet up with Simmons on time.

She flinched, remembering a few days ago when she'd rushed to get away from Johnny. On the way out, she'd slipped on the stairway. Falling down several steps, she twisted her ankle and hit her face on the landing. Her cell phone must have fallen from her purse when she tumbled. She hadn't dared take the time to look for it. Anyway, for all she knew, it had broken in the fall. Instead, she'd just driven home. Now she wished she had a phone to call her sister.

Kelly's heart raced and her hands shook. She took a deep breath. Her emotions had to be kept under control, at least until she finished meeting with the FBI agent. After that, it wouldn't matter if she fell apart. She wiped a drop of sweat just before it ran down her neck and into her bra, then turned on the air conditioner. Her hand was shaking again.

A modest log cabin nestled in a small grove of birch trees at the shore of Lake Tahoe came into view as the Honda rounded the corner. She drove the car onto the gravel driveway and turned off the engine.

She knocked on the front door. No answer. She peeked into the garage window and saw a blue truck parked inside. Simmons must be home. Her knuckles hurt from rapping on the door. Annoyance ran down her spine. He knew she was coming to see him today. His truck was in the garage. Why didn't he answer?

Could he be hurt and unable to come to the door? She squinted and peered in the front window but couldn't see into the dark of the living room. No sounds emanated from the cabin.

Her hands turned cold as her blood raced from her extremities. *He must be dead. Stop. Don't let your imagination run away with you.* Instead of jogging back to the car, she stood on the front porch. She had to find Simmons and give him the flash drive so her nightmare would end.

Maybe he was sleeping. After all, he did work nights at the casino.

Just then a dog barked. She followed the sound to the back of the property.

From a wooden pier on the edge of the lake, a yellow lab came bounding toward her, wagging its tail. At the end of the dock, Simmons, holding a fishing rod, stood staring at her. He waved.

Thank God.

"Hi, Ted." She smiled at the forty-something, average-height, and average-weight man with brown hair and eyes, the generic Caucasian male. Perhaps that's why he did undercover work. He was so ordinary, so forgettable. Just a guy you'd see anywhere and not pay attention to him.

"Ted, I'm so glad to see you," she shouted. Everything was okay. Her horrendous situation was almost over. "It's beautiful out here on the lake." She walked toward him.

"Yeah, fishing's good too, and the house is comfortable. I don't usually get such a plush assignment."

The Labrador circled her demanding she pet him. She scratched his ear. He continued to wag his tail.

"His name is Yeller. Not original, but he doesn't seem to mind." He patted the dog's head. "I'll be right back."

He jogged to the end of the pier and picked up his tackle box and then returned. "Let me stow this gear and toss the fish in the fridge. Then we'll get the flash drive. Can we take your car?"

"Okay, sure."

Kelly sat in the driver's seat and waited for Ted. She pushed down her impatience. It'd take about twenty minutes to reach the hiding place. In less than an hour, it'd be over and she could go home. She and Carrie would be out of danger.

Fifteen minutes later, the sky darkened, the wind blew off the lake, and the air turned cold. How long did it take to put the fish and tackle away? Maybe he was going to clean the damn fish before he came to the car.

Women have a bad rap for always making men wait. But lately, she'd been forced to wait, first for Brick at the casino and now for Ted.

She got out of the car and was hit by a gust of cold wind. She stood and let it cool her hot temper. *Calm down, it's almost over.*

At the front of the cabin, she banged on the door. "Damn it, what's taking so long?" She rubbed her hand and couldn't bear the thought of hitting it again.

The handle of the front door turned easily. The drapes were still closed when she entered the living room. She left the front door open to let a ray of sunlight penetrate the shadows. Even so, it took a second for her eyes to adjust to the dimness. Decorated in pine furniture with plaid upholstery, the room appeared homey.

"Ted, where are you? Are you ready to go?"

Silence.

She moved down a short hallway into the kitchen. An odor of fish assailed her. The open refrigerator door lit the shuddered room. The trout lay on a platter in the middle of the kitchen table. Ted's fishing pole leaned against the wall near the back door. He was nowhere in sight.

She started to shout his name but stopped. A shiver ran through her. Sudden fear warned her to keep quiet. She backed out of the room into the hallway.

For the first time, she noticed the hall door open to the garage and she could see the fender of Ted's truck. A shuffling sound came from the room, then the distinct sound of the garage door opening. She relaxed. Ted was in the garage. Maybe he'd decided to take his pickup truck. She walked quickly toward him.

145

"Ted, I went through the house. Do you want to take your…"

"Run Kelly, ru…

The intruder's knife sliced Ted's carotid artery, cutting off his words. He dropped to his knees holding his throat, blood sprayed through his fingers as he fell face down on the cement floor.

Frozen in shock, Kelly watched a river of Ted's red blood flow toward the open garage door. Her stomach retched. No one could lose that much blood and live.

The intruder who'd attacked her in her home glared at her. A bloody knife in his hand, he lunged for her. Just then, the dog came into the garage and ran toward the man and the killer tripped over Yeller.

At her car, she fumbled to get her keys out of her jeans pocket. Finally opening the door, she jumped in and started the engine. Grinding the gears, she struggled to force the car into reverse. The auto jumped and spit gravel from the back tires.

The killer yanked open the driver's side door. Her foot popped off the clutch. The engine died.

Chapter 17

The killer grabbed Kelly, yanking her so hard they both fell onto the driveway. He grunted as her full weight landed on top of him. As she struggled to stand, he grabbed at her ankle. She kicked him in the groin and ran down the long driveway toward the road, praying she'd reach the road before he caught her.

Brick's car pulled onto the property. His side window was open and he leaned out and shouted, "What the hell are you doing here? You promised to stay at your cabin."

"Simmons is dead. I saw the killer." Bile rose in the back of her throat. She glanced back toward the house. The assassin was gone. She came to a halt next to Brick's car and gulped for air.

"Kelly, go to your car and get out of here."

He didn't ask who Simmons was. Instead, Brick ran toward the house.

"We can't just leave Ted lying in the garage, dead," she yelled and then swallowed hard.

He paused. "I'll have the FBI take care of him. Get in the damn car and go!"

She walked on wobbly legs toward her old Honda.

Too late to help Ted, but his dog was alive. She couldn't leave him to starve.

She ran toward the house.

When she entered the garage, Brick was nowhere in sight. Was he chasing the killer?

With some trepidation, she glanced around the room. Yeller lay near the agent's body. The dog's tail wagged when he saw her, but he didn't leave his master's side.

Her stomach rolled and tears blurred her vision when she saw Ted face down in his blood.

"Yeller," she called to the dog. His tail continued to wag, but he refused to move. Finally, she went to him and pulled on his collar. "Come on, boy. Come home with me. Don't worry. I'll see your master's taken care of." She wiped a tear from her cheek. "You're going to be okay."

"Kelly, what the hell are you doing? I told you to get out of here?"

Brick was alone and breathing hard. "Take the dog and leave."

***

Back in her cabin, Yeller lay on the floor near the foot of Kelly's bed.

Was there someone from Agent Simmons' family who'd want to take care of Yeller? Did Ted have a wife and children who'd mourn him? She gulped back a sob.

Brick would find out.

What was she going to do about the flash drive? It was still hidden. Without Ted, she didn't know who to trust. She never should've taken it. Damn, Simmons for talking her into grabbing it in the first place. *Oh God, what am I thinking?* Trying to do the right thing, the man died.

She sat on the bed and sobbed. Yeller went to her and put his head in her lap as if to comfort her. She patted his head. "I know you're sad too. Aren't you, boy? Don't worry. We'll find Ted's people and take you home." She rubbed his ear. "If they can't keep you, you'll stay with me." *If I'm still alive.* He licked the tears from her face.

Maybe she should leave the flash drive in its hiding place and hope no one finds it. *Not a good plan.* The intruders said she'd die if she didn't return it. She pictured Ted, blood gushing from his neck wound. She wouldn't let him die in vain and she didn't intend to be the next one murdered.

Her head ached. Her stomach growled. Hunger was proof she was still alive. It felt like a betrayal of Ted Simmons to want food. She groaned. *Don't think anymore.*

After a quick shower, she hurriedly put on a white cotton shirt, a short jean skirt, and black flats.

Brick was waiting for her in the dining room. He was probably pissed.

"You look lovely," he said when she entered the room.

"Uh—thanks." She didn't feel lovely. She felt numb. How could he even think of saying something like that after what they'd seen this afternoon? She gazed into his clear, steadfast eyes. Was he trying to keep her calm?

There was no criticism in his expression. She'd expected to see a reprimand for leaving after he told her to stay. She sat at the table. "Brick, how did you find me?"

"I put a tracking device on your car."

"You didn't trust me."

"Did you deserve my trust?"

She flinched and turned away without answering.

"I made dinner."

"I can't eat." She swallowed hard. "I thought I could, but thinking of Ted, there's no way."

"You have to. Everything's ready." He waved at the food on the table, then pulled out a chair and sat down.

149

The aroma of the meal wafted to her. Still, the thought of eating sent a wave of nausea washing over her, then her stomach growled.

Without conversation, he plated her food, Caesar salad and barbecued chicken bought, along with a bag of dog food, at a market on the way back to the cabin. He sliced the famous San Francisco sourdough bread. It was trucked in every day over the mountain pass when Donner Summit wasn't snowed in, He put a slice on her plate. She found a bottle of Napa Valley Chardonnay and opened it.

He refused the wine. She filled her glass. "After the events of today, I need it". She hesitated. "You're sure the FBI will find out who killed Ted?"

"Yeah, it doesn't matter how long it takes, the assassin is going down."

She took a bit of chicken and ate a few bites of lettuce, washing it down with the wine.

He ate everything on his plate.

Stunned that he could eat as if today was just another day at the office, she took another gulp of wine and swallowed slowly. Maybe it was a normal day for him, but not for her.

Ted's death seemed to heighten her senses and made her aware of how short life was and how quickly it could be snuffed out.

Her feelings for Brick intensified as well. She stared at him. He'd changed his clothes and was now wearing a blue dress shirt. It emphasized the color of his eyes. What would it feel like to run her fingers over the soft fabric of his shirt and feel the taut muscles that lay underneath?

A jolt of guilt hit her. She was surprised to discover the proximity to Ted's death caused her to need to prove she was still alive. Making love to Brick would do that.

150

Shattered Rules

In the living room after dinner, he started a fire in the fireplace and then sat in a wingback chair across from the sofa.

A glow from the wine swirled in her. She leaned back on the sofa, still holding the half-full glass of wine she'd brought from the dining room. Determined to recover from the horror of the day, she sipped more of the white wine. She'd probably had too much of a good thing at dinner and would pay for it in the morning. She didn't care. How many evenings were left before the intruders killed her like they murdered Ted?

One night to remember, that's all she wanted and, because of the timeline of the intruder's threat, it would have to be tonight.

Brick scrutinized her, his eyes stopping where her denim skirt ended. She looked up to see the firelight flashing in his eyes, unreadable emotions flared, and then his eyes narrowed. He turned away before she could decipher their meaning.

Could he be experiencing the same craving that was pulsing in her? A hope that he might yearn for her as much as she hungered for him made her brave. *I'll show him just how much I want him.*

The log in the fireplace flared and sent sparks flying. He rose to stoke the fire and added another log.

"Sit on the couch with me," she said, surprised by the sound of passion in her voice.

"I'm fine." He sat in a chair across from her.

"It's lonely over here."

"Looking beautiful as you do right now, you don't make it easy to say no."

"Then say yes." She held out her hands.

"There's no use denying I'd like to. I can't. Nothing in our situation has changed."

151

"Make love to me." She pretended she hadn't heard his words.

"You've had too much wine and too much stress. Be sensible."

"I don't want to be sensible. Just once, I want to make passionate love to you and let tomorrow take care of itself," she whispered.

A perplexed expression spread across his face, but desire soon replaced it and a fire burned in his expression.

"Brick."

"Kelly, you've got to be practical. If I took you tonight, you'd regret it in the morning."

"No, I wouldn't. If I'm practical, where does that get me?"

"You're young. What's the hurry?"

"The intruders tell me I won't live to see next week, let alone my next birthday."

He cringed.

"I want something to show for my time on this earth." She drank the last drop of wine and put the glass on the coffee table. She adjusted her shirt and tossed her hair back from her face. "I want you. Don't be afraid, I'll be gentle." She giggled.

His lips remained firm, even though a smile shone in his eyes. "I can't give you what you want."

"Yeah, you can. I want you to take me. I don't want a commitment, no strings, and no plans for the future. Maybe tonight is all I have."

"Don't talk like that."

She stood up and went to him. Just a breath away, she whispered, "Don't turn me away. Can't you see how much I need you?"

He opened his mouth to answer and she kissed his open mouth, tongue to tongue.

He pulled away. "Kelly, stop."

She glanced down and saw his need grow. On her tiptoes, she reached up to kiss him again and said, "I know you think you're doing the right thing by pushing me away, but you're not."

She held his face and kissed him again. His hands were at his side, his body unyielding. Nonetheless, she continued to kiss him, her hands running through his hair and down his taut backside.

Finally, with a groan, he wrapped his arms around her and pulled her closer.

She clung to him. Since she was a teenager, she'd wanted him, only him. She'd feared there'd never be a chance. This was her opportunity. She wouldn't let it go.

Her breasts pressed against his hard torso. His muscles tensed. She arched her hips to get nearer to him. His breath caught and his need came to full attention.

He tore his mouth from hers. "We shouldn't be doing this."

Instead of answering, she undid the buttons on his shirt and ran her hands over the warm skin of his chest, then moved downward. His abdominal muscles flexed as she continued to experience the planes of his hard body while her tongue licked his tightened nipples. She gazed up to see raw hunger reflected in his eyes. Was it a manifestation of her need or was she seeing his hunger?

"I could do better if I had a little help," she whispered before kissing him again.

He seized her and kissed her hard. She moaned as the intensity of his kiss filled her. He forced his tongue deep into her mouth, and she opened wide to accept it. He drew her firmly against him, making her move with the rhythm of his shifting body.

His fierceness surprised her. Maybe he wanted to scare her away, but instead, her need flared. She met his demands with demands of her own. His stubble rubbed against her skin. She didn't care.

He yanked on the snaps of her shirt and they popped open one at a time. Then he released her breasts from their pink satin and lace restraints. Her nipples hardened, begging for his touch.

His mouth found one and sucked on it.

"More." She sighed, holding his head to her. Sensations only he could make her feel coursed through her. The love for him she'd been hiding surged. Heat burned within her and she thought she'd ignite.

His persuasive hands explored her, following her natural contours. He moved downward toward her core. "Yes, yes," she said, her breath ragged.

His mouth reclaimed hers as he touched her inner thigh. She clung to him, trembling.

His staccato breathing echoed in her ear, sending a shiver of eagerness through her. Rational thought was lost, and only emotion remained. Her body quivered in anticipation.

Their movement and breathing became harmonious, a single rhythmic motion, building toward a crescendo. He was in charge now and she willingly let him guide her toward release.

The doorbell rang.

"Who can that be?" Kelly struggled to catch her breath.

"Don't know. You better go into the bedroom," Brick whispered in a husky voice. "I'll take care of whoever it is."

The doorbell buzzed again.

He tucked in his shirt and went to answer the door.

Shattered Rules

She grabbed her shirt and ran from the room.

In the bedroom, her body still ached for Brick's touch. She looked in the mirror, her face was flushed and her lips were swollen.

She sat on the bed, closed her eyes, and tried to bring her breathing under control.

Who could be at the door?

Chapter 18

Brick looked through the peephole in the cabin's door. A thirty-something, uniformed, California Highway Patrol Officer stood waiting.

"Officer?" he said as he opened the door.

"Are you the owner of this property?"

"No. I'm visiting."

"Is the owner available?"

"I can get her if it is absolutely necessary."

"It is."

"Do you have some identification?"

The officer held out his badge and gave Brick his card.

"Thanks, Officer Mullins," he said. "I'll be right back." He left the officer standing on the porch.

On the way to the bedroom, he saw Kelly coming down the hall toward him. "It's a highway patrol officer. He wants to talk to the owner of the cabin."

"Why?"

"I don't know. Go find out. Play it cool. Don't offer any information. Give short answers to his questions, then stop." He looked down at her and could see she was still tipsy. "If he asks about me, tell him I'm a friend. Don't tell him I'm an FBI agent."

"I don't see why, but if that's what you want." She shrugged.

"And don't let him in the house. Talk to him on the porch. If he needs to come in, he can get a search warrant."

***

She switched on the porch light and went out to introduce herself. Brick stood at her side.

"Hello, officer. How can I help you?" she asked. Her voice was a whisper.

"There's been an accident on the highway. A young woman is badly injured."

"No!" She grabbed Brick's arm.

He held her close.

"Are you all right, Miss?" Officer Mullins frowned.

"Yeah." She pulled away from Brick. "Please go on."

The officer stared at her for a second, his eyes narrowing as he searched her face. He yanked a small pad of paper and a pen from his pocket. "As I was saying, there's been an accident and a woman's been seriously hurt. Looks like a hit-and-run. The odd thing is, there was no ID on the woman or in the car. We're still searching, but the only thing we've found so far is a scrap of paper with your address on it."

"This address?" *Carrie wouldn't need the address to a house she'd been going to since she was a kid.*

"Were you expecting anyone?"

"No, that is—uh." She faltered under Officer Mullins' stare. "Well, no I wasn't."

"I have a favor to ask Miss. Take a look at this photo. He on my phone. It's the young woman I told you about. I have to warn you she's none too pretty right now. Her face hit the steering wheel when her car crashed. But if you know who she is, it could help us find her family.

She's going to need them." He handed her the smartphone.

A woman on an ambulance gurney stared at her. The female's face was puffy and disfigured, her eyes swollen shut, no way to see their color. Her short brown hair was matted with blood.

Kelly recoiled. With her hand to her mouth, she pushed down the nausea rushing up her esophagus. She shoved the phone at the officer and turned away.

Brick reached for her or she would've fallen.

"I don't know her." She choked out the words. Guilt for being relieved that it wasn't her sister filled her.

"You've got no idea why she'd come to see you?"

"No. I've never seen her before."

"Take another look. Maybe a name will come to mind," Officer Mullins held his cell out to her again.

She didn't want to see the photo again, but the woman needed help. If it had been her sister, she'd want someone to identify her. With a deep breath, she squinted and took a closer look. Something familiar caught her eye. There was a butterfly tattoo in a spider web on the woman's arm.

"Oh, God! It's Amanda." Kelly gasped. "She's changed her hair again, but it's Amanda Owens."

"You know her?"

"We go to the same school, the University of Nevada in Reno. She was my roommate. The last time I saw her she had black hair with a blue strip. I didn't recognize her until I saw her tattoo."

"You said her last name is Owens?"

"Yeah."

The officer wrote it down on his notepad.

"Can you tell me how to reach her family?"

"I don't know, but the university should be able to tell you."

"Of course."

"I can't imagine why she was coming to see me. We're not friends, just roommates."

"Many roommates become friends," Mullins offered.

"True." But not after all that had happened between the two of them. Still, there was no reason to say that to the officer.

"Thanks for the information."

"I'm glad I could be of some help. Will she make it?"

"Too early to say."

"I pray she'll be all right."

The officer smiled for the first time, making him appear younger than he had when he first arrived at her door.

"Could I see her?"

"She was unconscious when I left the hospital."

"Maybe someone could call me when she wakes up. I hate to think of her being hurt and alone."

"I'm going back to the medical center tonight. I'll ask the staff. What's your phone number?"

She gave him the cabin's number and he wrote it down.

"I'll be off." He shoved the notepad into his shirt pocket.

She stood on the porch and watched him drive away.

"Why would Amanda come here? What did she want?"

"Maybe she was short on funds and thought she could score some more easy money by selling you information. Looks like that's how she made her living, peddling info, a very dangerous way of life."

She gazed up at Brick's severe expression. "I feel sorry for her."

"You have a kind heart." His expression softened, leaving him devastatingly handsome.

"I hope she lives long enough to learn from her mistakes," he said. "A little freak heading down life's highway in the wrong direction, if I let myself, I could feel sorry for her. I'm not going to."

"For a moment I thought it was Carrie. God help me, I was glad when I knew it was Amanda and not my sister. I'm so ashamed."

She remembered her roommate's purple and swollen face. "I'm going to be sick." She ran into the cabin.

***

Brick stood at the front door watching Kelly race toward the bathroom. *Too much wine.* He went back outside and watched the waning evening light and breathed in the crisp pine-scented air.

If Officer Mullins hadn't arrived when he did, he'd have made a terrible mistake. He'd lost his objectivity. Always proud of his self-discipline, being around Kelly had caused him to struggle to curb his emotional impulses. It was nearly impossible to manage his physical response to her.

Her kisses were still fresh on his lips. With a deep breath, he fought his desire and pushed down the memory of touching her. His feelings were a complication he hadn't expected, didn't like, and didn't need. He couldn't let his guard down again or he'd be unemployed, his ass kicked out of the Bureau. He made a promise not to react to her again. Now he had to find the strength to keep it.

In the living room, he saw a shimmer of pink on the green carpet, Kelly's bra. The satin fabric felt sensuous to his fingers, he allowed himself to savor the feel of it. A flash of fever roused him. For the last time, he let his hand run over the satin and recalled the sensation of touching her breasts.

Holding the bra gingerly in his left hand, he carried it to her bedroom. The door was open. He set it on the dresser. The adjoining bathroom door was closed. "Need any help?" he shouted through the door.

"Go away."

"You're sure you can manage?"

"I'm fine. Leave."

"Okay."

"Go."

He made his way to the upstairs bedroom and sat on the king-sized bed. What had come over Kelly? Stress must be getting to her. There were a lot of ways to relieve tension, but if he could help it, making love to him wasn't going to be one of them.

There was no denying she tempted him, his body's reaction to her was proof of that. Even now, just remembering what happened tonight, his body hardened. He exhaled deeply.

He wasn't a schoolboy who couldn't control his craving. She'd ignited his veins with flowing lava, but he wouldn't take her when she'd had too much to drink. If he ever did make love to her, it'd be when this case was over and with both of them clear-headed, knowing exactly what they were doing.

What was he thinking? He grunted. She was off limits.

He called the Truckee Forest Hospital. There was no change. Amanda was still unconscious. The hospital would notify him when she woke up.

Had she been on her way to see Kelly to score more cash? Or could she have told them something useful about this whole mess?

First Ted Simmons was murdered, and then Amanda was attacked. Someone was playing hardball. It had the earmark of a clean sweep, clearing away anyone who could stop whatever was coming down the pike. Kelly would be next. If Amanda lived, maybe she could give them a sliver of information that would help keep Kelly alive.

He was about to turn off the bedside light and get some sleep when his phone rang.

"Yeah."

"Haven't heard from you," Don said.

Brick hackled at the implied criticism from his boss. "Anything new?"

"Not yet, Don." He considered telling him about Amanda but didn't. The fewer people who knew where to find her, the safer she'd be. "How about you? Anything on your end?"

"Nothing."

Don was holding something back. He could hear it in his voice. "By now there must be something coming out of the woodwork."

"No," Don said, irritation deepening his voice. "Brick, don't cross-question me. Concentrate on doing your job. Kelly knows something. Men wouldn't be after her if she didn't. She's playing 'Miss Innocent' for you, but she's pulling your chain."

Don was quick to brand her a criminal. Would everyone feel that way?

"Something's going down. I've got chatter on the line and Jack Anson is dead. Brick, I want answers yesterday."

It was the perfect time for Brick to mention Ted Simmons' death to Don. Something he couldn't define stopped him.

"I need answers," his boss continued. "No more Mr. Nice Guy. Push the girl and get me something. If you don't, I'm going to bring her in and question her. She won't like it. I want answers. Got it?"

"Understood." He tried to keep the anger out of his voice. His boss' superiors must be pressuring Don and he was putting the screws to him.

"Brick get me something in the next twenty-four hours or it's out of my hands. I'll have to bring her in."

"I hear you." He bit back expletives and disconnected the phone. Pushing Kelly to deliver information she didn't have didn't help anyone. What the hell was wrong with Don?

He thought about how little information he'd discovered during his time with Kelly. They hadn't learned anything new in days. "Shit." All he'd turned up were dead ends. Useless anger burned in his gut. If he couldn't get more information, how was he going to defend Kelly?

***

The intruder parked the truck in the same place he had parked the SUV last night.

His hands itched. He scratched them hard enough to leave deep red lines on his skin. Again, he decided the pain was better than itching. Restlessness stirred in his veins. Hunger for another kill grew in him. Starved, he couldn't wait much longer to feed again.

If it was up to him, he'd kill the guy, grab the girl, and have done with it. But it wasn't his job to decide what to do. His job was to follow orders. That's why he was the best. He never overtly questioned orders. He merely carried them out. When the time came to act, he would. But because this was his final job before retiring and returning to his homeland, he was finding it hard to wait.

163

***

Johnny Vega's stomach growled. He sat in the dining room of the penthouse suite. Waiting for the room service breakfast to arrive,barefoot and still in his maroon silk pajamas, he put his elbows on the glass table and cursed his chef for getting sick. He had enough trouble. Today he couldn't even get a decent meal. His head throbbed, too much liquor last night.

Damn, Kelly. When she took the flash drive, she put him in a hell of a spot. Mr. Yi was breathing down his neck waiting for the delivery of the flash drive. If he didn't get it back soon, his ass was going to be in a ringer. His men had better find her or he'd make sure their ass was in that ringer along with his.

He recalled the day he met Kelly. A college student, she'd seemed so sweet, and innocent, but damned hot. Not only that, he liked her. With women, that didn't happen. He used them and when he grew tired of the bitches, dumped them. For the first time in his life, he cared about a woman. He trusted her and even thought of marrying.

He groaned. Not since the death of his mother had he felt loss. Without Kelly, there was a cold void of loneness in him and he didn't know how to fill it. He remembered the way she looked, smiled, and moved. He could almost feel the softness of her skin and smell her sweet vanilla scent. His need for her grew. "Bitch."

He'd evaded relationships, but she'd blindsided him. She caught him off guard and he'd let her see a secret part of him no one, except his dead mother, had seen. He'd nurtured Kelly, cared for her, and loved her. She rewarded him by stealing the guidance system.

Shattered Rules

If she'd been in the room, even though he knew it would be like killing a part of himself, he'd have murdered her with his bare hands.

***

The morning light hurt Kelly's eyes. She turned away from the bedroom window. Her head throbbed. It served her right for drinking so much wine last night.

When she thought of her behavior, her cheeks burned with embarrassment. She moaned as much for her foolish actions as for her aching head. When was she going to get it through her dense brain? No matter how much she loved him and no matter how kind he was to her, Brick didn't love her.

Coming on to him, she must have seemed pathetic. If only she could do last evening over. All she'd wanted was a night to remember. Well, now she had one. *Fool.*

How could she face Brick in the harsh morning light?

Chapter 19

Kelly returned from the bathroom carrying a glass of water, set the tumbler on the bedside table, and reached for an aspirin bottle. The telephone rang. As she rushed to answer it, the glass of water fell off the nightstand, soaking the carpet.

"Damn! Hello."

"Ms. Shaw?"

"Yes."

"This is Mrs. Page from Truckee Forest Hospital. Officer Mullins said you wanted to be advised when Miss Owens was awake."

"Yes."

"She woke early this morning."

"Can I see her?"

"Well, you would have to check at the nurse's station, with the accident and all. But since the officer said it was okay with him, if you wanted to visit her for a few minutes, I guess it would be okay."

"Could I come this afternoon?"

"Anytime, before eight o'clock tonight."

"I'll be there and Mrs. Page, thank you for calling."

"You're welcome, dear."

Shattered Rules

With a bath towel, she soaked up the spilled water. She quickly dressed in blue jeans, a powder blue T-shirt, and her white running shoes.

Relieved to know Amanda was awake, she sighed. Visiting hours might be until eight tonight, but she wanted to get to the hospital as soon as possible. Her roommate might slide back into a coma before she had a chance to talk to her, then she'd never understand what Amanda wanted to tell her.

With a deep breath to give her the courage, she left to go and find Brick. Would he mention her stupid behavior from last night?

He stood in the great room looking out the window to the lake. "Hi," he said, barely looking in her direction when she entered the room.

"Hi," she answered. Completely conscious of his masculinity, she strained to control her desire to touch him. She steeled herself, waiting for him to make some remark about last night.

He didn't say anything else, didn't even ask how she was feeling. Grateful, she stood next to him and gazed out the window. "Amanda's awake. I'd like to go see her as soon as I can."

"No problem." He faced her. "Eat some breakfast and then we'll go."

His voice was controlled and distant, speaking to her as if she were a stranger.

Disappointment spiraled in her.

Truckee Forest Hospital, a seventy-five-bed medical center, was housed in a modern nondescript two-story building.

She hadn't been in a hospital since the death of her mother. The thought of entering the building caused her stomach to retch.

167

Though her father had died instantly in a train derailment, her mother had survived, lingering for days in the hospital. She'd stayed at her mother's bedside until her mom succumbed to her injuries. The feelings of hopelessness she'd experienced on the day of her mother's death returned.

Her hands tingled. Slowly she pulled open the heavy glass door and walked into the lobby. Amanda was the only one who had information that could help her get out of her situation. She had to see her before it was too late.

Brick followed her into the medical center.

The clean white lobby was devoid of the usual hospital odors and was about as welcoming as any medical building could manage. A gift shop stood near the front lobby. Even though she was in a hurry to see Amanda, she entered the shop.

With a bouquet of mixed flowers, a card, and two fashion magazines, she paid the clerk. She refused Brick's offer to pay and insisted on using her credit card. She wasn't about to be more beholden to him than she was already.

The volunteer at the information desk told them Ms. Owens was on the second floor, east wing. They were to stop at the nursing station and ask for her room number.

The walls of the second floor were painted mustard yellow and smells of various chemical and human substances wafted out of the patients' rooms as they walked by the open doorways. Swallowing hard, she ignored them.

Brick wore a stoic expression as he moved quickly toward the nursing station. Was this the first time he'd been in a hospital since his recovery from injuries he received almost five years ago?

About halfway down the hall, a twenty-something woman, dressed in an aqua uniform, sat alone at the nursing station desk.

"May I help you?" She smiled.

"We'd like to see Amanda Owens," Brick said.

When Amanda's name was mentioned, a shadowed look came over the young woman's face.

"I don't know." She consulted her papers.

"Sorry, no visitors allowed."

"Oh. Thanks anyway."

He pulled Kelly with him as he left the nurse's station.

She opened her mouth to protest, but he gave her a quick shake of his head. They walked silently toward the exit.

"I got her room number," he whispered.

"How?"

"As the clerk ran her hand down the list of patient names, her finger stopped for a second at a room number and then continued down the page. Come on," he said. "We'll go see her."

They waited until the young woman at the desk turned her back to them, then walked quietly back down the hall toward Amanda's room.

"Let's see if anyone's standing guard," he whispered. "I hope there'll be an officer watching her room."

The door was open and the sign next to the door said, "Owens, No visitors." No police officer stood guard.

"So much for protection," he said. "I know the California Highway Patrol, with the recent budget cuts, is short-staffed, but I'd hoped the local police would've been brought in to help protect her."

He glanced around the quiet hallway. "You go in. I'll stay here at the door."

"What do I say to her?"

"Just say hello and give her a chance to talk. She was coming to see you. She must have had a good reason."

***

The white walls of Amanda's room were cold and uninviting. A mini blind did its best to decorate the window. A ceiling fixture gave out light but did nothing to heat the room.

Kelly rubbed her arms for warmth.

The first bed was empty. Amanda lay in the bed next to the window. She didn't move and for a moment, Kelly thought she was unconscious again.

Visions of her mother lying lifeless in a hospital bed came unbidden to her. She swayed under the weight of the somber memories and steadied herself by holding on to the nearest wall.

She glanced at Amanda, but instead of seeing her, a vision of her mother saying, "Be a good girl. Don't let me down."

She swallowed and covered her mouth to stifle an anguished cry. She'd failed her mom and let her sister down too. Now she'd even hurt poor Amanda.

"Is someone there?"

"It's Kelly."

"Hi, Kell."

Amanda's voice sounded surprisingly strong compared to the way she looked. Her usually pretty face was unrecognizable, swollen eyes were almost closed and the skin around them was a deep purple. With a bandage on her nose and a splint on her arm, she looked small and as pale as the white sheets of the hospital bed.

"I came to see how you're doing."

"Okay—I guess."

"I brought flowers and a couple of magazines." She put the magazines on the bedside table, but with Amada's eyes so swollen she probably wouldn't be able to read them.

"Thanks."

"Maybe I can find something to put these flowers in."

She discovered a green glass vase, the kind given out in florist shops, in a cupboard. She took it to the bathroom, filled it with water, and put the vase of flowers on the windowsill. "There, that's better."

Amanda looked toward the window and squinted.

Could she even see them?

"Nobody ever gave me flowers before."

Kelly gasped. "Well, I'm glad I'm the first." She tried to sound cheerful and managed an unfelt smile. She reached for Amanda's hand and gave it a light squeeze. To her surprise, the woman held her hand for a moment, before letting it go.

"Is there someone I can call? A family member?"

"No."

The answer was so firm and final. She didn't ask any more on the subject.

An awkward silence followed.

"He tried to kill me," Amanda finally said.

"What!"

"He wanted to murder me. It wasn't an accident. The driver drove right at me. His car pushed me off the road."

"No!" It was so close to what had happened to her during the snowstorm, the night her Honda was almost run off Donner Summit.

"I was coming to see you. You helped me get my car back and I wanted to help you."

Amanda shifted her position in the bed, winced, and took a slow breath before speaking again. "You took something from the man my boyfriend was working for.

Those guys said they were going to get it back, even if they had to kill you."

"Johnny Vega?"

"No, some other dudes. There was this Asian guy. I think he's a Korean dude and some man from the government. My boyfriend was supposed to work for them, but he backed out. You met Norm. He doesn't scare easy. But these men scared him real bad."

"You mean someone from the U.S. Government is after me?" She paused. "Amanda, that doesn't make sense."

"Norm said somebody in the government is out to get you. That's all I know. But I'm scared and you should be too."

Ted Simmons was from the government and he died protecting me. Amanda must have the facts wrong.

"It's hard to talk." Her roommate moaned. "My mouth is so dry."

There was a plastic pitcher on the bedside table. Kelly poured a glass of water, then helped Amanda sit up and take a sip.

"Kell, whatever you took, give it back. It's not worth dying for. They'll kill you as sure as I'm sitting in this hospital bed."

"Oh, God!"

Amanda lay back against the pillows. "I'm tired," She slumped in the bed and closed her eyes.

"I'll let you rest."

"Will you come and see me again?" Her eyes blinked open.

"Of course, if you want me to." Kelly gazed at the bleak, sparsely decorated room and shivered. "Is there anything I can get you before I go?"

"I can't watch TV. You have to pay for it and I don't have my purse. It must be in my wrecked car." Tears squeezed out from the woman's puffy eyes, wetting her bruised skin, it dripped down her gaunt cheeks. "I just have to sit here and look at nothing."

How could the roommate see anything with her eyes almost swollen shut? Still, Kelly's heart squeezed. "Don't worry. I'll have them turn on the TV for you. You helped me. I'll help you." She smiled. *What are credit cards for?* Later, she'd worry about paying the debts she was racking up.

"Thanks, Kell."

"No problem. I'll come back and see you soon."

As she was leaving, a nurse entered the room.

"Didn't you see the sign? No visitors."

She rushed out of the room without answering. As she left, she heard Amanda ask for pain medication.

Brick was down the hall talking to Officer Mullins. She joined them.

"The Doc said Miss Owens is in guarded condition," the Officer explained. "She's got a broken arm, broken nose, a cracked rib, and a probable concussion. They're watching for internal bleeding. She's going to require plastic surgery. But all and all, she's damn lucky to be alive."

"What happened on the highway?" Brick asked.

"Hit and run. She doesn't remember too much about it. Can't tell us what kind of vehicle hit her, but something smacked her car so hard it sent her compact over the embankment. Up on the ridge, it should've dropped at least thirty or forty feet. But someone up there was watching out for the little lady." He pointed upward. "She was above the tree line. Hard to believe her auto found the only pine for miles on that embankment. The compact was wedged between the slope and the tree stump, preventing the car from going down the cliff."

"I'll be damned," Brick said quietly.

"She's a little bit of a girl, but somehow, she managed to get out of the car, crawl back up to the road, and wave down a motorist. Good thing a car came by soon after the accident. The driver called 911 and stayed with her until the ambulance picked her up. Yep. She's one lucky lady."

"And you have no idea who did it?"

"Nope. She was the only witness, not much traffic on the road at that time of day. With that bump on her head, she can't tell us much. We may never know exactly what happened." Officer Mullins' eyes narrowed. "The doc said there's less than a fifty-fifty chance she'll remember." He shook his head. "I'd like to get my hands on the jerk who did it to her." He paused. "We can't solve them all. She's alive, that's what matters."

"Right," Brick agreed. "But damned aggravating they might get away with hurting her."

"The police will continue to look, but..." He shrugged.

"Thanks for the info."

"No problem." Officer Mullins walked down the hall toward Amanda's room.

On the way out of the hospital, Kelly stopped at the information desk and asked that the TV be turned on in Amanda's room.

Back in the sedan, she leaned against the leather seats and closed her eyes.

"You okay?"

"Seeing Amanda brought back all the memories of seeing my mom in the hospital just before she died."

"Memories can be cruel." Brick touched her hand. "Let's go to the cabin."

174

Chapter 20

Kelly didn't speak on the way back to her cabin, glad Brick didn't require conversation. In her emotional state, she couldn't focus.

When they arrived, she entered and checked for messages—nothing from Carrie. She dialed her sister's cell phone again. No answer.

With the portable phone still in her hand, she gravitated to the back deck. Lake Tahoe lapped serenely at the edge of her property and a cool breeze drifted off the water. She sat in a deck chair facing the lake.

Brick joined her, a can of cola in his hand. He sat in the seat next to hers and stretched out his long legs. "Want a sip?"

"No thanks."

He gulped the soda.

"Brick, I was just thinking. When Agent Simmons asked me to take the flash drive, he led me to believe that it had something to do with gambling." She rubbed her temples. "Then James told us Johnny said I'd taken his system." She paused. "Besides computer systems, how many different kinds of systems are there?"

"Uh, gambling, surveillance, alarm, information and guidance systems." He paused. "That's all I can think of."

"I understand gambling systems, but what would Johnny do with any of those other ones? I can't make sense of it."

Brick shrugged. "We're missing some information. Why don't you tell me everything you know again? This time don't leave anything out."

She held her breath as she recalled Ted's warning about talking only to him. But he was dead. She exhaled and glanced at Brick. "Can I trust you?"

His eyes narrowed and then darkened.

"I'm sorry. I shouldn't have asked that. But Ted Simmons died and I'm so afraid I could say the wrong thing and cause the death of another person."

"Kelly, you didn't cause his death."

The heat beat down on her. Perspiration beaded on her forehead. She wiped it away. Brick was trying to help her. "I'll tell you everything I know." A sense of release spiraled through her as she explained all she could recall. "That's all I know."

"And Amanda said someone in the government is after you?"

"Yeah."

"If a government official wanted you, all he'd have to do is call or go see you and present his identification. The government doesn't send men to threaten you with dying and ransack your house."

"I took Johnny's flash drive, so I assumed the intruders were his men. Now I don't know what to believe. Damn. I wish I'd had a chance to ask Agent Simmons questions." Her throat tightened and she wiped a tear from her cheek. "I can't believe Ted's gone."

"You okay?"

"As good as I can be—considering."

Shattered Rules

"Amanda told you there was a Korean involved and I saw an Asian man in Johnny Vega's office. What would a Korean national be doing in Vega's office?"

Before she could answer, he said, "It's a rhetorical question. I don't expect you to know." He ran his hand through his hair. "I'm just thinking out loud."

She sat back in the chair and turned her face toward the sun. "It's so peaceful here on the lake with nothing but the sounds of the trees rustling in the breeze. I can't believe…"

"Kim Yi Jun, that's the name. It just popped into my head."

"What?"

"That's the name of the man I saw in Vega's office. Of course, it's probably not the man's real name or the name he's using now." Brick put his empty cola can on the picnic table next to him.

"Years ago, I was in the Army and stationed in South Korea, when a news story broke." He frowned. "I guess it didn't get much media attention in the States. He paused. It was a big story in Seoul. A South Korean businessman had been caught selling restricted electronic parts to North Korea. His photo was on the front page of the newspapers and the TV news. He disappeared before he could be arrested. Well, he has just reappeared in Reno, Nevada, in Johnny Vega's penthouse."

"None of this makes sense," She shifted her position in the deck chair and faced Brick. "What does that man have to do with Johnny and the flash drive I took?"

"Good question. Wish I had the answer. My question: What the hell is he planning to do in the US?"

"I wish I understood." She leaned back and closed her eyes.

**

Brick watched Lake Tahoe lapping the shore just a few feet from the cabin's back deck. *Damn.* He needed time off. This was the perfect place. Too bad this wasn't his vacation.

His phone rang. He recognized the number. A woman who worked at the phone company was returning his call.

"Hey, Liza, how's it going?"

"Don't take a two-year-old on a camping trip." She laughed.

"I'll file that for future use." He laughed too. "Got anything for me?"

"The number you wanted me to check is a cell phone, part of a group of phones belonging to In-Tech, located in Redwood City. The report goes to the national headquarters of the company, but the end user gets a copy of the bill and I have his name, address, and credit card number if you want it."

"The name and address will do." He pulled a pen and a scrap of paper from his pocket and wrote down the information. He'd put it in the smartphone later.

"Thanks, Liza, you never let me down. Kick your husband in the pants for me and tell him he owes me a round of golf."

She laughed again. "Don't be a stranger. Come to dinner when you get back."

"Will do."

He picked up the can of cola and started to drink, then remembered it was empty. He crushed it and threw it into the trash can next to the chair.

"Kelly, I have one more phone call to make."

He called the FBI office and asked for Maryann. Would she check on George Nicholas Nickels? It was the name of the man Liza had just given him.

Shattered Rules

He'd never heard of the company In-Tech. What did they do? Obviously, something high-tech. Was it involved in hardware or software? His father would know. An early software developer in Silicon Valley, his dad was aware of most of the companies and their CEOs, if not in person, at least by reputation.

He hadn't spoken to his dad for months. They butted heads more often than not. Most interactions with his father ended in an argument. He cared about his dad, but all too often it was easier not to see him. Still, he couldn't think of anyone else who could quickly give him the information he needed.

He punched in his father's private number. A sense of remorse hit him for calling only now when he needed information.

"Hello," a deep voice said.

"Dad, it's Brick."

The line was silent. Finally, Dad answered in a gruff voice, "Son."

"I have some FBI business to clear up and thought you might be able to help."

"If I can."

Brick heard disappointment sounding in his father's voice. "Dad, what do you know about a company called In-Tech?"

"That's a name I don't hear very often."

"Really?"

"In-Tech keeps a low profile. Other companies are building a brand to increase their name recognition and have their names on glass and steel monuments across Silicon Valley. In-Tech's buildings are nondescript structures in various parts of the valley, Mountain View, Redwood City, even as far south as Campbell."

"Do you know what they do?"

"It's all pretty hush-hush. Most of their work is for the Pentagon. The CEO is ex-military. Rumor has it that In-Tech is working on a new long-range missile guidance system, with a computer chip so accurate, it could send a missile into your morning cup of coffee without making a splash."

Brick tightened his grip on the phone.

"Unless the man was bragging to me," his dad continued. "if missiles were placed strategically throughout the country, a United States missile could land almost anywhere in the world."

Brick's back muscles knotted. In the wrong hands, the system could be placed to send a missile anywhere in the States.

"Brick, did you hear me?"

"Yeah. Good info. Thanks."

"Don't be a stranger. Your mother would like to see you."

"I won't."

"And Brick?"

"Yeah."

Dad cleared his throat. "Never mind."

"My love to Mom." Brick broke the connection.

Shit. He should have said my love to *you* and Mom.

When this case was over, he'd try to mend his relationship with his dad. He forced stale air from his lungs and took a deep cleansing breath.

Could the system Kelly took be a plan for a top-secret long-range missile guidance system? The thought of her being involved in a theft of that magnitude was beyond his imagination. But he was now being forced to envision the unthinkable.

He glanced at her in the deck chair next to him. Her eyes were closed and her expression was peaceful. He was reluctant to wake her. No choice. He grunted. "Kelly, wake up."

He related the new information and watched the blood drain from her face. Good thing she was sitting down. He doubted she'd be able to stand.

"Johnny couldn't have anything to do with a theft from a high-tech company. He's a gambler and a thug. He doesn't comprehend anything about high-tech." He doesn't even use a computer." She hesitated. "I was a fool to have anything to do with him, but espionage? I don't believe it." She sat straight up in her chair. "The idea is crazy."

"I find it hard to believe too, but those are the facts." He held Kelly's gaze. "Something has happened and Johnny's in the middle of it."

"I don't—I." She paused.

"In-Tech must have several layers of security. Only an insider could arrange a theft like that. Someone with top-secret clearance." Brick rubbed his chin in thought, then stared at Kelly to see her reaction.

"If there'd been a theft wouldn't we have heard about it? It'd be on the TV news and make newspaper headlines all over the world."

"Not if company officials don't know there's been a robbery or if the US government doesn't want anyone to realize it."

"How could that be possible?"

"Kelly, the system would be in encrypted files and only a person with a password could access those. What if one of the insiders say one of the designers of the system, was willing to sell the plans? He could make a copy on a flash drive. No one would be the wiser."

Brick thought for a moment. "Or if the owner of the company is greedy and wants to make money from other governments, not just from the US, he could—" He stopped, not wanting to consider the possibility.

"You think Johnny Vega somehow got a copy of the military plans from In-Tech and that's what's on the flash drive I took?"

"Could be."

"I don't believe it." She shook her head. "Okay, I broke the rules by getting involved with Johnny. But this is more than I bargained for." She stopped then said, "I remember Agent Simmons told me something about US security." Her voice trailed off into silence and she put her head in her hands.

Finally, she looked up. A distraught expression spread across her face. "When I took the drive, I was trying to do a good thing and make up for my mistake in getting involved with Johnny in the first place. Now Ted's dead and Carrie could be next. I guess it's true that no good deed goes unpunished."

"Don't." He moved closer.

"That's the way I feel. How am I going to protect Carrie? Maybe I should give the drive back to Johnny."

"You're not serious. If there are plans for a US missile guidance system, you can't let Vega have it again. You don't want it to go into enemy hands, do you?"

"Of course not, but if I don't Carrie will die. I thought you cared about my sister."

"I do, but I have to look at the big picture. We're talking about the safety of our country."

He thought of the intruder's promise that Kelly and Carrie would die if she didn't return the flash drive. The men would keep their word as sure as they killed Ted Simmons. Brick had to do something to stop them before the Shaw sisters ran out of time.

182

Chapter 21

Brick watched Kelly walk to the end of the deck and face the water of Lake Tahoe. A breeze rustled her hair, sending out golden sparks of light. She held on to the railing, her face turned to the wind, a petite figure alone against the tides of nature. The royal blue sky turned to steel gray. Waves kicked up by the wind made white caps on the lake. A flurry of birch leaves skittered across the plank floor of the sundeck.

If only he could stop time and keep her safe. A realization spread through him. She'd become precious to him, more important than anything else in his life, his job, his future gone from his mind. She permeated his soul, a dazzling, shimmering presence. He only wanted to protect and cherish her. Instead, he feared circumstances beyond his control would cause her death.

He stood behind her and kneaded her shoulders to release the tension he found. He thought she might pull away. Instead, she leaned against him.

"I've always loved it here on the lake. It's so peaceful and filled with so many wonderful family memories."

His arms encircled her.

"When my mom and dad died, everything went to hell. At first, Carrie and I quarreled, then we didn't speak. I had nobody I could talk to. At that time, I met Johnny and he made me feel important, even loved. He was exciting." Breathless, she paused. "Thinking about it today, I realize that I became a rebellious teen after my parents were gone. I was angry at the world for taking my family away." She gulped back a sob.

He waited for her to continue.

"I was horrible. I made Carrie's life miserable. Now, because of my recklessness, I've put her life and your life in danger."

"Don't, Kelly."

"Friends warned me against getting involved with Johnny. I was too pig-headed to listen. I'm guilty. I've caused so much trouble. I'd give anything to change the past."

"Hush." He wanted to stop her agony. How well he understood her feelings of guilt. He'd felt the sting of it. If only he'd known of his partner's betrayal, he could have prevented Annie's death, the witness he was supposed to protect.

"What a complete and utter failure I've been." Kelly's voice was just a whisper barely heard above the wind in the trees.

"You're too hard on yourself. How could you know what Johnny was like?" He pulled her closer and stroked her hair. "There was no way to foresee any of this."

She turned, her breasts grazing him as she did, and buried her face against his chest.

Another gust of wind blew off the lake and she trembled.

"You're cold. We should go inside," he said, not wanting to let her go.

She raised her head and gazed at him. "Kiss me. Please."

Slowly, he gently brushed his lips against hers.

184

She moaned.

Smoldering heat ran through him, a feeling like nothing he'd experienced with any other woman. even though he understood he had to let her go soon, he kissed her again, deeper this time. "We better go inside." He took her hand and led her out of the wind to the safety of the living room.

***

Kelly watched Brick light the logs in the fireplace. When he finished, she went to him. "I love you. I always have. Even when I was a teenager, I loved you." She reached up and covered his lips with her fingertips. "I had to let you know. You don't have to say anything. It's only that I've been saying it to myself for so long, I wanted to tell you, just once."

His eyes widened and then his expression softened.

With a gentle hand, she caressed his cheek. The past and the future were unimportant, nothing mattered but this moment. It was the only thing that held meaning for her. She wanted him more than she could admit. From now on, whatever happened between them, some part of her would always love him.

"Come here, Kelly."

She went willingly and he lifted her face to his and gazed into the depths of her eyes. There was raw hunger in his expression, the same hunger enflaming her.

"I don't deserve you, Kelly." His voice was ragged.

He'd always exuded such strength. So, when he bent to meet her parted lips, she was surprised by the gentleness of his kiss. A charge went through her. She clung to him. Gone were her feelings of guilt and regret. Brick was with her. That was the only thing that mattered.

His caress sent a wave of pleasure spiraling in her. Her heartbeat quickened. She leaned against the length of him and opened her mouth wider, wanting more of him.

His kiss became more demanding. As their tongues danced, she met his passion with a passion of her own. His hips began a slow undulating movement and she went with him.

Her hand ran down the length of his corded arm. She took his hand to her breast. Nipples tightened at his touch and heat flooded the space between her inner thighs.

She wanted her skin touching his.

Almost as if he comprehended, he lifted her top over her head and dropped it to the floor. With one easy movement, he released her breast from the sheer satin fabric of her bra.

"You're beautiful," he whispered as he knelt before her and rubbed her nipple to hardness. With his mouth on her breast, he sucked, causing a wave of emotions deep within her. She sighed and held his head to her tingling breast. His tongue played with her nibble and her response was so intense she wondered if she could continue to stand.

He released her zipper and with one movement slid her pants and panties to the floor. He kissed her abdomen and left moisture to cool her flaming skin. His hand ran slowly down her body, caressed her thigh, and then touched her femininity. She moaned as her whole body quivered and her knees became weak.

He lifted her into his arms, took her to the bedroom, and set her on the bed.

On her back, she watched as he pulled his shirt over his head and tossed it away. She marveled at the golden skin that spread over his muscled torso, for the first time understanding the meaning of "hard body."

A need sparked in her. "I have to touch you, everywhere." She sat up and ran her palms slowly over his solid chest and abdomen. She heard his breathing quicken.

He undressed and his body spoke, with eloquence, of how much he wanted her. He was impressive and so much more than she could have imagined. His need stood fully extended in front of him.

"I want you," she whispered and then lay back down and gazed up at him, her arms stretched out to receive him.

He held himself over her, his body almost touching hers.

With just the thought of his contact, she quivered and arced up in anticipation. She reached for him, running her hands over his strong back and tight buttocks.

He straddled her as his mouth reclaimed hers. His strong hand kneaded her breast. Waves of sweet heat soaked her core. His mouth found her pearled nipple, while his fingers reached her center, touching her until ripples of longing pulsed through her.

Her blood turned to molten lava. It coursed through her veins, setting fire to a new part of her as it flowed, her body softening as it warmed. In anticipation of his entry, her pelvis rose to meet him. She wanted him inside her, pushing, demanding, and taking.

"Brick, please."

***

He gazed at the passion in her eyes. Her clear translucent skin and tightly budded breasts were tipped with moisture. Her slender legs open in welcome.

He wanted to plunge into her and take her with hard thrusts, until neither of them had the strength to continue, drowning her fire with his seed. But more than meeting his yearning, he wished to give her pleasure and wipe away some of the pain she'd suffered.

She looked so delicate. He didn't want to hurt her. He tested her to be sure she was ready. She sighed and clung to him.

"More," she whispered.

Little by little he entered her, the sweetness of her overwhelming. She moaned, almost undoing him. He shivered and it took all his control not to completely sheath himself in her.

He concentrated on pleasing her, kissing the nape of her neck while he rubbed her breast to hardness and then caressed her private spot until she begged him to penetrate her completely. She called his name and her hips jerked upward. Moving with her, he slid deeper inside, increasing in strength and speed until he filled her wholly. Her honey was sweeter than he thought possible.

***

Her breath caught as she felt him tight inside her. *Yes.* She didn't speak. She was too overcome with sensations of love. She wanted him to take her, fill the empty years she'd wasted, and fill the time she'd existed without him.

Her body and soul were captured and held by his spiraling need. Trying to pull him even closer, her nails scratched him as her hands ran down his back to his hardened muscles.

It only seemed to increase his desire. He moved faster, just as she wanted. She joined him, moving in rhythm as if they had been performing as lovers forever.

While he thrust inside her, he reached for her private spot and stroked it over and over again.

"Yes," she whispered.

The sensations were so great she didn't know if she could absorb them. Her breath was ragged and her skin inflamed. She welcomed his passion as he relentlessly thrust again and again, increasing the pace and tempo. She held on as he carried her with him, her body saturated with feelings almost too great to manage. Her mind was filled with love for him. He touched her once more and she shook and cried out.

Her control was gone, and her body moved of its own volition, passion captivating her. She heard herself cry out again as he thrust deeply inside her and she went still. A tingling sensation spread from her core throughout her body, even to the end of her fingertips.

He released his seed into her. "Kelly," he whispered.

Intertwined, she lay with him and listened to his ragged breathing and heard her matching breaths. Spent, but fulfilled, she smiled.

Minutes passed. She opened her eyes to see him rise on one elbow and look down at her.

"I cherish you," he said, gently putting his fingertips over her lips, letting her know she didn't have to respond. Then he rolled onto his back and pulled her with him.

Her head rested on his broad chest. With her ear to his heart, she listened to the resolute beat. More joy than she could imagine filled her.

Safe in his arms, she closed her eyes.

She woke, naked under the sheets. Her hand touched her swollen lips and then her budded breasts, the nipples still sensitive from Brick's kisses. It was true, and not a dream, he'd made love to her. She rolled over, expecting to see him in bed next to her. She sat up with a start. Her heart beat erratically. He was gone.

Chapter 22

The sound of the shower running in the bathroom caught Kelly's attention. Relieved, she lay back in bed and imagined Brick in the shower, soapy lather running down his muscled torso.

In the bathroom, she breathed in the masculine scent of shaving cream. She found him standing tall and potent in the clear glass-enclosed shower, steam swirling around him. His back to her, he rinsed his closely cropped blonde hair. Shampoo lather slithered down his powerful back.

He turned slightly and she watched as he took a bar of soap and made lather circles on his chest. Every sculpted muscle flexed. Heat exploded in her core as she imagined his competent hand bathing her.

What would it feel like to have him soap her breast? Her nipples tightened. It was so soon to want him again, but seeing him sent desire exploding, causing a quiver of anticipation. She had to touch him.

Without saying a word, she opened the door of the shower and entered. She used her fingertips to trace shampoo lather as it meandered between his shoulder blades and down to his firm buttocks.

His breath caught and he grabbed her hand.

She noticed his eyes widen as they tracked the warm water that dripped down the cleft of her breasts. He bent forward and licked the trail of moisture from her right breast. His hand claimed it while his mouth descended to suck her nipple to hardness.

His need grew before her as his masculine power engulfed her. Hot liquid surged in her. She rubbed her skin against his, gliding across his soapy body. There was no friction, just delightful sensations, reminding her of silk.

Only he could fill her yearning. She forgot where she was and it didn't matter if the water was warm or cold, he was with her. Her nails dug into him, demanding he take her.

He gave in kind, sending his long fingers hard inside her, while he tenderly kissed her neck. She groaned and leaned against his strength. Her legs became putty.

He easily lifted her to him and her legs went around his hips so he could enter. Leaning against the tiled shower wall, he steadied her and with one swift push entered her fully. She gasped and felt explosive feelings as he expanded her. She kissed him, her tongue dancing with his. He pumped into her, rotating her hips to meet his as he lifted her up and down to meet his thrust.

She was sore from the earlier love-making, but it didn't stop her from moving with him, wanting everything he could give and arcing to bring him closer. Finally, she cried out and clung to him while waves of sensation flooded her.

His thrust increased and his muscles tightened as he released life-giving fluid into her. Then he held her tenderly to him. Her legs were still around his hips, her head rested on his shoulder.

He carefully lowered her to the floor. The water was cool now, but she was still hot. She sagged against him, waiting for her breathing to slow and her self-control to return.

With a soapy washcloth, he washed her, ever so gently, touching her core. She shuddered and he kissed her waiting lips. He rinsed the soap from her body and turned off the water.

Moisture clung to her skin. He wrapped her in a bath towel, carried her to the bedroom, and placed her on the bed.

"Rest my sweet." He pulled the bedding around her and then returned to the bathroom.

Safe and warm under the down comforter, blissful sleep overtook her.

***

Brick wrapped a towel around his waist and returned to the bedroom. He gazed at Kelly sleeping in the bed. Her full lips were parted, blonde hair framed her face and the top of one pink breast peeked out from under the covers and begged to be caressed.

He wanted nothing more than to slide under the sheets next to her and let her softness envelop him. But problems were building, events he might not be able to stop. Deadlines loomed. Lying in bed with Kelly wouldn't protect her.

They'd been thrown in the middle of something neither fully understood. He'd better find answers before it was too late. Now that he'd experienced Kelly's love, the thought of her death sent a jab of pain to his gut. He had to prevent it.

At some point, he'd have to tell her he'd returned to investigate Johnny Vega. He'd make sure she understood his love was separate and that it had nothing to do with the current mess with Vega.

Shattered Rules

A sense of remorse shook him. He should've had more self-control and waited to make love to her until she was aware of his assignment with the FBI. But he'd longed for her since the first day he'd seen her in bed at the Redwood City motel.

Today, three times, she'd asked him to take her. With the threat of her demise hanging over her head, he knew there might not be another chance for them to be together.

He recalled Annie's young face, the witness he'd been unable to save. Even though five years had passed, her eyes still haunted him. He tore his gaze from Kelly, then dressed and left the bedroom. He'd make damn sure she was defended. He would succeed in protecting her, even if he died doing the job.

In the living room, the flames in the fireplace were dying embers. His body heated remembering Kelly standing nude in front of him. Backlit by the flames of the fireplace, the fire's glow had turned her blonde hair to pink, the color of her rosy nipples. Her skin had shimmered smooth and evenly tan in the firelight, her hazel eyes filled with love. He groaned. When she knew why he was with her, would there be loathing in her eyes?

He retrieved his cell phone from a table near the hearth. He had a text message from Maryann in the FBI office with facts on George Nickels, the man who'd paid Amanda for information about Kelly. Nickels had entered the country on a temporary work visa. His native country was Greece. He worked for In-Tech. Though it was unclear what he did for them. His work visa expires at the end of next month. The man's description: thirty-five years of age, six feet four inches tall, and a hefty two hundred and sixty-five pounds, with brown eyes and black hair.

Why would a foreign national be hired at a high-tech company with United States defense contacts? What expertise could he have that couldn't be found in Silicon Valley?

He dialed In-Tech and asked for George Nickels.

"Mr. Nickels is in Reno on business. He won't be back until next week. Would you like his voicemail?" a woman asked.

"Yeah, thanks."

Brick listened. It was the same voice message he'd heard when he called the phone number Amanda had given him. He disconnected without leaving a message.

So, Mr. Nickels was in Reno. Brick rubbed his chin and wondered if the man had anything to do with Amanda's accident and Agent Simmons's death.

Nickels fit the description of the first intruder to enter Kelly's house, tall, muscular, with dark eyes, black hair, and wearing a signet ring with an initial "N." Was the intruder Mr. Nickels? Maybe he dared to wear the signet ring because no one knew him. He was a stranger from offshore.

The man told Kelly she'd die the day after tomorrow. If Nickels was the intruder, the bruises he had given her were just healing. Brick would be damned to hell before he let Nickels get a chance to touch her again.

He relaxed his fisted hands and thought about the facts. He had names: Johnny Vega, George Nickels, and Kim Yi Jun, an American with known ties to organized crime, a Greek working for a high-tech company in Silicon Valley, and a Korean who illegally sold electronic parts to North Korea. How were they linked? It didn't make sense.

It was disturbing that no matter how much he understood, he still didn't have enough information to make sense of the situation.

He stared out of the window. The beauty of Lake Tahoe had disappeared in the fading light, night had arrived.

There was another call to make. Don would be feeling pressure from his superiors to get concrete data. He hoped the name of George Nickels, at In-Tech, would placate Don and the FBI bosses.

The phone rang once and his boss picked up the call. Without preliminaries, Brick gave him the name of George Nickels. He told him about his concern that blueprints from an In-Tech long-range guidance system might have been stolen.

His boss didn't comment, but Brick could feel the man's tension. He and Don had been friends for years, but now the warmth of that friendship was gone and uneasiness had replaced it. What was going on? The only explanation he could think of was Don felt the weight of his responsibility.

"If there's a flash drive out there with plans for a guidance system, we better give the CIA a heads up." Brick paced as he spoke. "Nickels is a foreign national and Greece is close enough to the Middle East to make my hair stand on end."

Silence.

"Don, are you still there?"

"What else do you have for me?"

"I put a name to the sketch I sent you. The man's name is Kim Yi Jun, a Korean. I don't know what he's calling himself now. That was his name when I was stationed in the U.S. Army in South Korea. He was caught selling restricted electronic equipment to the North Koreans. At the time, it was front-page news."

"The South Korean police didn't apprehend him?"

"No. He just disappeared. I guess that he high-tailed it to North Korea. You can imagine my surprise when I see him sitting in Johnny Vega's conference room."

"You're sure it is the same man?"

"Yeah, it's him alright. My hackles are up. Something is about to happen. The shit's going to hit the fan. The CIA needs to be told."

"Nickels, Yi, and their goons killed an FBI agent. They will pay for leaving my agent face down in the Truckee River. And I heard about Agent Simmons bleeding to death in his own home. Nobody is taking this case away from me," Don shouted. "As far as I'm concerned, the CIA has bumbled one too many cases. They've left this country vulnerable while bogged down in their internal politics. I'm not going to give them a chance to bungle this one. We'll handle it. Clear!"

"As glass." Brick didn't like it, but he'd been given a direct order. "Crystal clear."

"I want any new info you have as soon as you get it. Stay in touch." Don demanded. "And buddy."

"Yeah."

"Remember to watch your back."

The phone went dead in his hand. He groaned. Don's decision not to tell the CIA was one they would regret.

Chapter 23

A delicious feeling spread through Kelly. Being with Brick had been more incredible than she'd imagined and her daydreams had been breathtaking. With her yearning for him fulfilled, for the first time in her life, she was complete. Brick cherished her.

Later that evening, they dined on Swiss cheese sandwiches and green salad. Then they sat together on the sofa in front of a roaring fire and drank decaffeinated coffee. He put his arm around her and she rested her head on his shoulder. The flames danced in the fireplace as she remembered the ballet, they had danced together that afternoon.

Everything that was needed to be said between them had been said. With no verbal communication necessary, she sat in contented silence. She was happy to be in his company.

"Let's go to bed," he said.

Vanna grinned because this time he meant together. "Can't wait."

The next morning, dressed only in Brick's navy polo shirt and her black bikini panties, she stood in front of the old gas range cooking scrambled eggs. A pitcher of orange juice sat on the kitchen table and pancakes were being kept warm in the oven. She'd promised to have breakfast on the table by the time he had showered.

They'd made love again during the night, slow tender love, and woke each other's arms.

A whiff of shaving cream entered when Brick walked into the kitchen. The masculine aroma, mixed with the smell of pancakes.

He wore jeans and the dove gray shirt he'd worn the day he came back into her life. She'd feared him then. She should have understood there was no need.

"Hmm, smells good," He kissed her. "Oh, and the food smells good too." He winked.

Vanna laughed, poured coffee into a mug, and handed it to him.

"That polo shirt looks a lot better on you than it ever did on me." He pulled her to him, hugged her, and then covered her neck with kisses.

"Brick, the eggs will burn." She giggled and slipped out of his arms to save breakfast.

"Hmm, eggs the way I like them." He licked his lips.

"I'm glad."

"Aren't you going to eat?"

"You're all I need." She kissed him on the cheek.

"The men I called to install the security system will be here soon." He took a bite of the eggs. "You should get dressed. You look great, but I won't share you with anyone."

"Okay. I can take a hint." She wrinkled her nose and then grabbed her coffee cup and started to leave the room.

"I thought all you needed was me."

"You and a cup of coffee."

She quickly showered and dressed in white Capri pants and pale pink cotton tee, and white running shoes. Then she returned to the kitchen.

Brick was taking a cola from the refrigerator. He popped it open and swallowed a gulp.

"You drink too much soda." She pretended to scold him.

"My one vice." He chuckled.

"Brick."

"Yeah."

"I was thinking about the Asian man you saw in Johnny Vega's conference room. You believe he's here to buy Johnny's flash drive with the plans for a missile guidance system on it."

"That'd be my guess."

She went to the sink and started to wash the breakfast dishes. "Shouldn't we tell someone that Mr. Kim is here in the Reno, Tahoe area?"

"The FBI realizes. I told my boss, but so far, the man hasn't done anything illegal. All the authorities can do is watch and wait." He grabbed a towel and began to dry a dish.

"I read a news article about nuclear bomb testing in North Korea." Vanna put a wet dish on the drying rack. "I didn't pay much attention, though I recall when the leader, Kim Jung Un, came into power. TV journalists talked about what he might do, follow his dictator father's path or go his own way. But living in the US, it didn't mean anything much to me."

"I'm afraid it didn't mean much to most people. The Democratic People's Republic of Korea, DPRK, North Korea to you and me, is a mystery." He grabbed another dish. "For years, countries wondered if they were testing nuclear weapons. Of course, now everyone understands they have intercontinental ballistic missiles and nuclear weapons and they continue to test missiles."

"Yeah, but didn't Kim Jung un, and the last US president agree to "work toward" denuclearization?

"North Korean leaders have promised to do that at least twice before."

"They didn't follow through?"

"No."

Kelly shook her head as if overwhelmed. "And now?"

"Good question." He paused. "It appears there are multiple secret sites and the North Koreans have increased the production of fuel for nuclear weapons. It seems, the leader has no plans to denuclearize. Instead, Kim is growing bolder firing many ICBMs recently. Not only that, he has made it clear the missiles could strike the US and anywhere else in the world.

"No way! How can you be so calm?" She didn't expect him to answer. An FBI agent must talk about weapons of mass destruction as a common topic of conversation.

Contemplating the new information, her hands trembled. The soap bubbles from a dish she was washing dropped to the kitchen floor unnoticed. "Does the United States know how many nuclear bombs the North Koreans have?

"Well, from what I've read, we have a good idea." He shrugged. "But who can say?"

"And they can't be stopped?" She handed Brick a wet dish.

"There are sanctions on the country already, but they go around them with the help of the Chinese, Russia, and Iran. However, short of a war, it's hard to influence an isolated country run by a dictator that's often secretly supported by other governments."

He dried the dish and set it on the counter with the others before putting them into the cupboard, then turned to face her. "With an accurate longer-range guidance system, the North Koreans would be guaranteed to hit their exact target, the Senate, the Pentagon, the White House."

"My God! Why would they do that?"

"I'm not saying they would. But they're a desperately poor country and almost isolated from the rest of the world's commerce. They have trouble getting the needed equipment to continue building more nuclear weapons." He took another gulp of cola. Silent, he sat at the kitchen table.

"Kelly, the question is: Would they strike the United States or try to extort the government by promising not to use the missile guidance system?" He shrugged again. "Worse, they might sell the system in the underground weapons market. If a rogue nation got hold of it, they could send a bomb against any nation in the world."

She gasped and looked out the window at the beauty of the surrounding Sierra Nevada Mountains. Strong and silent, they jutted toward the azure sky. In the Tahoe Valley with its gray granite walls acting as a fortress and the lake as a moat, she'd always felt safe. But now she realized security was an illusion.

With the dishes forgotten, she sat at the kitchen table next to Brick and let out a sharp breath of air. "I can't believe we're having this conversation. It's too hard to think I'm involved, even peripherally." She hesitated. "I used to read about world events. I barely gave them a passing thought. Today, I'm thinking I might have a flash drive with information on how to build a long-range missile guidance system that could send a nuke to kill millions of innocent people and destroy cities all over the United States." Kelly paused. "I can't get my head around that."

She gazed into his clear eyes, "Why would other countries want the delivery system? It would bring the wrath of the US military on them."

He leaned forward in his chair. "Imagine if all rogue nations and terrorist organizations, large and small, bought nuclear bombs. They still couldn't deliver them past a short range, perhaps a few hundred miles. So, even with nuclear bombs out there, most of the world feels pretty good."

Brick pushed a hand through his hair and took a slow breath. "If a long-range guidance system was on the open market, it would change the balance of power in the world and give parity to the rogue nations against the major powers."

"I…" her voice cracked. She cleared her throat. "It can't be true."

"The only way we'll know for sure is to find the flash drive and take a look at the files."

"I don't want to deal with this. I…" She ran from the room.

***

The phone rang as she entered the bedroom. She grabbed it in time to hear Brick say hello.

"Brick."

"Don, why use the house phone? My cell phone is safer."

"I want to be sure where you are."

"Ask. I'll tell you."

"Have you learned anything more from Kelly?" Don said, ignoring Brick's statement.

"Not yet."

"You have twelve hours to obtain something I can use or I'll bring her in and interrogate her."

"Come on, Don, she's told me everything she knows. Interrogating her isn't going to help you."

"When I assigned you to see her, it was to get information on Johnny Vega. I didn't care what you did to get it. Well, you've been playing house with her for days and you don't have anything to show for it. She knows what's going down. Find out or I'm coming there and taking charge of her." The phone went dead.

"Shit," he said into the phone before he disconnected the call.

She carefully hung up. He'd been assigned by the FBI to come to her house. She'd let herself believe he had returned to see Carrie, but he'd stayed because he cared for her. Stupid.

Yesterday, she told Brick she loved him. Yesterday, he'd said he cherished her. Today, she felt the sting of his lies. Remembering her behavior in the shower with him, her cheeks burned with embarrassment. He'd let her behave like that, knowing she was just another assignment.

He'd probably have a good chuckle behind her back. How did he keep from laughing in her face? A cry crawled up the back of her throat. *Damn him.*

Brick was in the foyer saying his goodbyes to the men who had installed the security system in the cabin when she found him. "I trusted you. How could you?"

"What are you talking about?" He closed the door behind the men.

"I heard your telephone conversation with Don. You came to my house to use me and get information on Johnny Vega. You've never cared about me."

"Let me explain." He reached for her.

"There's nothing to explain. It is all too clear. You were willing to do anything to extract intelligence. Even make love to me. You know what that makes you."

"Don't."

"I trusted you!"

He reached for her again, holding her to him. "I never meant to hurt you, Kelly, but you need to calm down. Becoming hysterical isn't going to accomplish anything. Give me a chance to explain."

"Let go of me."

Brick's composed voice annoyed her. Why was he always so calm? She wrenched out of his grasp. "I don't want your explanation. I've heard too many of your lies."

"Try to understand. I had a duty to perform, but I never meant to hurt you."

"I had faith in you. I loved you," she whispered. "You took advantage of my trust. I didn't think you could be so despicable. I didn't think I could be such a fool. I hate myself for being gullible, but most of all, I detest you for using me."

He flinched as if he'd been slapped. His eyes narrowed and a grim expression spread across his taut features. She turned her back on him.

"I work for the FBI and I have responsibilities. That doesn't change my feelings for you. Grow up, Kelly. This is a serious business and our problems don't count for much."

"My feelings are all I have. And I don't care about your responsibilities."

"Stop."

"How dare you tell me what to do? You don't have the right, not after what you've done."

"Talking to you is pointless until you calm down." He left the room, slamming the door behind him.

Shattered Rules

She groaned. He said he cherished her. *Liar.* She couldn't stand to be in the same house with him. She grabbed her car keys from the entry hall table and ran out the front door.

***

The man watched the girl's car pull out of the garage. She was on her own and finally on the move. Was it to get the flash drive? He damned well hoped so. He waited for a moment and then followed, keeping the pick-up truck back far enough so it wouldn't be noticed.

Chapter 24

After driving aimlessly, Kelly found herself in Truckee in the Tahoe Donner subdivision. She parked on the shoulder of the road overlooking the closed ski lodge. Serene and beautiful, the lodge was a counterpoint to her disordered life.

With no cars parked nearby, it was good to be alone. She rolled down the window and took a slow breath. Resting her head on the steering wheel, she let out a sob.

The brisk air began to cool her anger and her breathing became more normal. At this higher elevation, lacy snowflakes floated to the ground. She looked up to see a delicate flake hit the compact's windshield. Soon others followed. Hard to believe there was snow in the summer.

With a deep breath, she forced herself to grab hold of her emotions. She refused to think of Brick's betrayal. Her life had disintegrated into chaos. However, sitting alone in the beauty of the mountains, even without Brick's help, she would survive. She didn't understand how, but determination was half the battle, wasn't it?

If she could go back to college, she'd take simple pleasure in learning and she'd do it without personal relationships. How little joy she'd received from personal entanglements, with first Johnny and now Brick. They'd only brought pain. She closed her eyes and strangled a sob. She'd give almost anything to return to the boring but safe life she'd lived before she met Johnny Vega.

"Kelly, you're dead."

Through the open car window, a pistol was pointed at her head. Fear surged and she began to shake. Completely absorbed in her thoughts, she hadn't noticed the other vehicle or heard the man get out of it and walk to the car. Her heart raced when she glanced from the gun to the man holding it. He was one of the intruders who'd ransacked her house. Gun in one hand, the other hand on her door handle, in one swift movement, he opened the driver's side door and yanked her out.

"Time to die."

"No!"

He hit her with his pistol and laughed.

She screamed.

"Shut up."

She shrieked and twisted her arm to release his grasp. He raised his hand to hit her again.

"Hey, leave her go." A huge man, wearing a blue plaid jacket and jeans, jumped from his truck and rushed toward them. "I said let go of her!" the stranger yelled.

The intruder stared at the Good Samaritan, then fired. Blood squirted from the man's chest onto the blue jacket he wore. He stumbled and dropped to the ground.

Kelly shrieked.

The shooter slapped her.

She screamed again. Her voice was hoarse, but she couldn't stop yelling.

He struck her over and over and pain radiated down the arm she held up to protect her face. Finally, she wrestled out of his clutches, turned to run, tripped, and fell to the ground.

He pointed the pistol at her.

"Don't kill me." She watched his trigger finger twitch and braced for the bullet's entry into her body.

Brick tackled the man.

She hadn't seen him arrive.

He punched the intruder. The guy grunted but still held onto the pistol.

They continued to fight. The men fell to the ground and rolled away from her and down a steep embankment toward the vacant ski lodge.

Terrified, she ran to the edge of the road and watched. At the bottom of the incline, they stood and exchanged blows.

The sky darkened as it snowed harder, making it difficult to see the men clearly. They both wore dark jackets and, from a distance, it was hard to tell Brick from the other guy.

One man got up quickly and pointed the gun at the other. The guy charged and fought for the weapon. The report of gunfire echoed in the mountain range.

A man dropped to the ground, and attempted to get up, but fell back and didn't move again.

Someone climbed up the embankment. If it was the killer, she should run to the car and drive away. But if Brick was shot, she couldn't leave him to die alone on the grounds of the ski lodge.

As terror filled her, a rapid heartbeat pounded in her ears. Transfixed, she stood waiting to find out who survived.

A man slowly crawled up the steep slope. Breathing hard, he stood at the top and glanced in Kelly's direction.

"Brick!" Relief surged through her. She ran to him, wanting to hug him, kiss him. But after the terrible scene in the cabin, she didn't dare. She stopped just before she reached him.

He caught his breath and brushed the dirt off his clothes. "Are you all right?" he asked, sounding as if he wanted to know.

"Yeah." Her face hurt and so did her arm, but she wouldn't worry him. "You okay?"

"I'm good."

"Is he..." She cleared her throat. "dead?"

"Yeah." His lips tightened into a thin line.

She shivered under his gaze. "A stranger tried to help me and he was shot."

She ran to the man and knelt beside him.

Lying on his back, eyes closed, he was still breathing. Tears of relief rolled down her face.

"You saved my life." She held his hand and he opened his eyes. "Thank you, mister."

He labored to take a breath and didn't speak. Instead, he squeezed her hand.

She said a silent prayer and pressed on his wound to slow the bleeding.

A police car, siren blaring and lights flashing, drove up and parked. Brick walked toward the officer who exited the vehicle. Another siren sounded and an ambulance came up the hill and parked near her.

"Excuse me miss," a young paramedic said as he knelt beside her. "We'll take over. It's okay. We'll take good care of him."

She stumbled as she moved out of the way. Wiping tears from her eyes, she trembled. Snowflakes changed her pink T-shirt to white. She gave up trying to brush the blood from her hand on her pants and instead watched the paramedic work on the stranger who saved her life. *Dear God, please help him. Let him live*

Brick came and stood next to her. He took off his jacket and put it over her shoulders. "We can go. Get in my car. I'll arrange to get yours later."

"I can't. I have to be sure he's okay." She nodded toward the wounded man.

Brick frowned. "The officer said we could leave. I showed him my FBI ID and he accepted my story. Let's get out of here."

She didn't respond, wouldn't look at him.

"I gave them your name and address. If we stay around, the authorities might want to ask more questions. I don't want to tell them any more than I already have. Right now, the police are concerned about getting information on the wounded guy. If we're still here after they have it, they'll turn their attention back to us."

She didn't move.

"Kelly, the paramedics will take care of the man. He's in good hands. Go to the car." His voice was calm but firm.

Depleted, she couldn't move. She'd taken as much emotional trauma as she could tolerate. Shocked, she couldn't seem to snap out of it.

"Damn it, Kelly. If we don't get out of here, we're both going to end up with our butts in the police station answering questions." He leaned closer. "If you won't think of yourself, think of Carrie."

She stared, then without a word, walked toward his sedan.

***

Brick turned the car around and drove toward the cabin. The attacker had wanted her dead, a cadaver lying face down on the side of the hill, snowflakes her only blanket. Instead, some poor guy seeing her beauty was struck with the bad idea of being a Good Samaritan. Now, he was fighting for his life.

The guy tried to protect her, but without expertise, he'd nearly paid with his life. Brick would be eternally grateful to the man. Without his intervention, Kelly would be dead.

He glanced at her. "I saw you drive away. A pick-up parked in the pine grove above the cabin started after you. That truck led me to you."

"I'm only breathing because you followed."

Their eyes met and undecipherable emotions flashed in hers. Did he dare hope she could forgive him for using her to obtain Johnny Vega's information?

He drove in silence to the cabin. He overrode the new security system and parked in the garage. In the kitchen, he watched her check the phone.

"No message from Carrie." She walked into the den and closed the door.

He could hear the sounds of the TV. Still, it wasn't loud enough to muffle her sobs. There was no point in going into the room. She wouldn't be comforted by his presence. Standing by the door, he listened until he could no longer bear hearing her sorrow.

He set the cabin's alarm system and climbed the stairs to his bedroom.

In the dark, a vision of the man he'd killed sent a spasm of grief through him. He'd been forced to take a life today. Were family members waiting for the man who lay dead on the slopes of the empty ski lodge? The question hung heavy on his mind.

He remembered Kelly's tears and her fear when the shooter pointed the gun at her. He groaned and pulled off his shirt and jeans and got into bed. Exhaustion racked his body, but scenes of the day played in his head. The sound of the pistol firing rang in his ears and the sight of the man dropping to the ground, dead, was seared on his retina.

At last, sleep came, but the dream that had tormented him for years began to run. He fought the familiar nightmare and struggled to wake up.

The noise of Annie's screams filled his ears. Again, he experienced the body-racking pain of bullets hitting his right knee, then the burn of a bullet grazing his temple.

As he fell to the floor, he turned to see Annie take a bullet in the chest. Bloodred splatter made a pattern on her white blouse. Disbelief shone on her young face as she dropped to the ground.

"No!" He shouted as he reached for her.

But this time it wasn't Annie. It was Kelly. Her white tank top turned red as her breathing squeezed precious blood from her body.

She lay just out of reach and he watched her blood as it comingled with his on the white marble floor. She beseeched him with her hazel eyes, begging for his help, her red-stained hand outstretched toward him.

"Kelly!"

He tried to wake up and shake off the nightmare. It wouldn't let him go.

In his terrible vision, blood dripped from his wound into his eyes. He wiped it away. Once more he attempted to move toward her. Retching in pain, he watched in horror as her beautiful young face grew pale. Each beat of her heart squeezed blood from her gaping wound. It dripped to the floor in rhythm with her breathing.

"No." He gasped and sat up. His chest heaved as his rapidly beating heart slammed against his chest.

Where was Kelly? He had to convince himself she was all right. He jogged downstairs to the den and quietly opened the door. Asleep on the futon, a crochet blanket covering her, she breathed normally. The muted TV sent an eerie blue light over her delicate features. He released his fisted hands, she was okay.

He had to keep her that way.

He entered the living room. The drapes on the window stood open to the pine grove that overlooked the cabin. Tonight, no vehicle was parked under the trees.

He relaxed.

***

Nickels parked a black truck next to an empty lot near the cabin. His signet ring felt like ice on his finger. *Another damned cold night.* The view from this angle wasn't as clear as it was from under the pines where vehicles had been parked for a couple of nights. Still, it was safer to move across the street, even if he couldn't see as well. His partner was killed at the ski lodge. It served the young kid right for letting someone get the drop on him. He'd never allow that to happen to him. The good didn't die young. The stupid ones did and he was one smart son-of-a-bitch. He scratched his cold hands and cursed the guy who was protecting the girl, itching to kill the man.

***

The next day the sun came up but gave no warmth. A thin layer of snow lay on the ground glistening in the light.

The intruder had promised Kelly would die today. All the same, Lake Tahoe lapped at the shore as it had for three million years when it was formed by geologic faulting. Today, nature caused no ruckus at the thought of the loss of another innocent. Life carried on as usual.

She bathed and dressed as she did every morning. Strange how calm she felt, like a soldier, maybe she was

213

becoming desensitized. Trauma didn't have the same effect it used to have on her. Because she didn't die yesterday, dare she hope she wouldn't die today?

The phone rang. *Probably Brick's boss with more bad news.* She had a few choice words she wanted to say to him. She picked up the receiver in her bedroom.

"Hello."

"Kelly, is that you?"

"Carrie. Thank God! Where are you?"

"I'm in LA at the airport. I missed my flight. I'm trying to get another one. If there's nothing today, I'll have to stay overnight." Her sister said. "But what the hell's going on with you?"

"Nothing."

"Something's wrong."

"It's a long story. I'll tell you when you get here."

"No. I got your cryptic messages. Don't go home. Why the hell not?"

"Carrie, do you remember when I asked you to hide a flash drive?"

"Yeah, I'm still waiting for you to explain that one."

"I asked you to put in the Thumb Dumb House."

"Yeah, sounded screwy to me, but I did it."

"Good. It was the only place I could think of that we both knew. I remember the day we gave the old mansion that nickname. Mom and Daddy were still alive. We had a lot of fun back then," Kelly said wistfully.

"The old place is empty and run down, Kell. Nothing's the same as it used to be."

"I know—never will be."

"Okay, what's this really about?"

"Carrie, I promise I'll tell you everything when I see you. I've got to go to the mansion. By the way, I need you to know that someone is out to kill me."

"What?"

"It's true."

"You're talking crazy, Kelly. I don't like it."

"I'm sorry. Please just come to the cabin as soon as you can.

"This is mad. I'm not going anywhere until you tell me what you've done."

"Nothing."

"Kelly, you can't fool me."

"Okay. I met a man." Kelly sighed. "I thought I was in love, same old story." She hesitated. "Johnny Vega was exciting. He's rich and handsome, but he's just pond scum. Anyway, I stole his flash drive. He took it from a government contractor and I was going to return it. Oh, it's such a long story and safer if you don't understand it. Carrie, just get here. I need to be sure you're safe."

"Now you're a thief. Damn, Kelly. You never follow the rules."

"It's not stealing. It's— so complicated." She rubbed her forehead and tried to ignore the ache forming over her right eye again. "I had to hide the flash drive from Johnny. I won't let him have it."

"What's on it?"

"I'm not sure."

"Shit. You stole it— only you don't understand what's on it? I don't have time for this nonsense. I'm hanging up."

"Don't. It seems crazy, but it's not. FBI agent Ted Simmons asked me to take a flash drive from Johnny. Agent Simmons said it was important to the government. I was going to hand it over to him. Before I could, he was murdered and now I don't know what to do or who to trust."

"Give it to the police?"

"No. The police and FBI have been infiltrated. I don't know who I can trust."

"My God, Kell, do you hear what you're saying? You're insane."

"Before I met Johnny, I wouldn't have believed either. But it's true." She pushed her hair back and put the phone to her other ear. "You've got to accept what I'm saying."

"You've gone bonkers," Carrie yelled. "Since Mom and Daddy died, I've tried to understand you and raise you to do what's right. I don't know where I went wrong, but I obviously did. Now you've gone off the deep end. You stay in the cabin and don't talk to anyone. Nobody. You hear me? Talk to no one. I'll see you there in a day or two."

The phone went dead in Kelly's hand. She didn't get a chance to warn her sister of the danger. It didn't matter. Carrie wouldn't have believed her anyway.

Dear God, please keep my sister safe

Chapter 25

Brick slammed the receiver down on the kitchen phone. He'd listened to the conversation and learned nothing. The Thumb Dumb house could be anywhere in the whole dammed country. He wanted to retrieve the flash drive without putting Kelly in danger again, but he couldn't. She'd have to tell him where the house was located. He'd bet, she'd demand to go or she wouldn't talk.

He wondered if she'd let him know Carrie had called. Or would she sneak out of the cabin to get the flash drive on her own? He was consoled by the fact that her car was still on the mountain road at the Tahoe Donner Ski Lodge. The keys to his car were in his pants pocket. But it would be just like her to, without a word, call for a cab and disappear.

He looked up when she entered the kitchen. Hair in a ponytail and dressed in white, she carried a pink fleece jacket.

Chilled by the reality that she could have died yesterday, he ached to hold her. She'd probably slap him if he tried.

"Morning." Her voice was pleasant, but there was no smile for him.

"Hi." A pressing question flashed. Now that an assassin was dead, who would be sent to complete the job of killing her?

He glanced at the jacket she held. "Going somewhere?"

She didn't answer. With a mug from the cupboard, she filled it with coffee and sat across the table from him, facing the window.

"About yesterday—how can I ever—" Her voice trailed away and moisture filled her eyes. "I want to thank you. I don't know how."

He watched her try to come to grips with her confused emotions as conflicted feelings registered in her expression.

"You saved my life. I'll never be able to repay you."

"You don't owe me anything." He moved toward her, then stopped, afraid she might flee.

"The water on the lake is rough today," she said as she gazed out of the window.

Darkness swirled beneath the foam and the waves crashed against the shore. He thought it was no more turbulent than his emotions.

Finally, she faced him again. "I got a phone call from Carrie. She missed her flight. She's still in LA."

"Did you tell her everything?"

"I tried. She thinks I'm crazy." She shrugged. "I need to use your car. I'm going to get the flash drive."

"You're not going alone."

"Yeah."

"Men have been paid to kill you! Don't you get it? You could have died yesterday?"

"I have to go." She trembled. "I'm not going to let Agent Simmons' death be for nothing."

"Think of yourself. You're still alive. Stay safe." It was the wrong thing to say, but it needed to be said.

"It's none of your business." She glared at him.

"Isn't it? I know how you feel about me, Kelly. You've made it clear you hate me." He forced the bitterness from his voice. After all, she was the one who'd been used and was still being used. "But if anything happened to you and I could've prevented it, I couldn't live with myself."

With her back to him, she stared out the window and didn't respond.

"Let me protect you while you get the flash drive. When that's done, you'll never have to see me again."

The thought that he'd never be with her again sent a grinding pain through him. Still, he'd suffered pain before and had learned to live with it. He could tolerate this because it was best for both of them. But her death, when he would defend her, was something he couldn't endure.

"And the FBI, what about them?" she asked.

"What do you mean?"

"You're here to do the FBI's bidding. I'm trying to do what Agent Simmons wanted, whether it's what your boss wants or not. How can I believe you wouldn't give the flash drive to the wrong man? One of Johnny's men."

"Good God, Kelly, I love this country. You can't honestly think I'd do anything that would harm the United States."

"No—no I don't. But you can't know who to trust in the FBI." Pain and loss were painted in her expression.

"That's ridiculous."

"Is it?" She closed her eyes and shook her head. "Agent Simmons said there were people in the Bureau that couldn't be trusted and now he's dead."

"Shit."

They sat silent.

Finally, he asked, "What do you want to do?"

"I need to get the drive and destroy it. Please don't stop me from doing what has to be done." She stared at him.

If he did what she wanted him to do, he'd lose his job, everything he'd worked for over the last few years, gone. Still, her beseeching expression tugged at him. Maybe she was right. What if the Bureau had been infiltrated? Was that possible? He hadn't thought so, but… They could destroy the drive and prevent it from getting into enemy hands.

"Okay."

"What?"

"We'll destroy it, Kelly, you and me—together."

"You mean it?"

"Since I joined the FBI, I've seen too much information go missing. if we destroy the flash drive, that can't happen to the plan for the missile guidance system."

He could imagine Don's angry reaction when his boss learned what they'd done. Better to explain it to him after the deed was completed and it was too late for anyone to stop them.

"Brick, can I trust you?"

"Yeah." The accusation hurt, but then what did he expect? Ever since they'd met again, he'd misled her. Of course, she'd be suspicious.

She glared at him, her expression so cold it sent a shiver through him. He wanted to close his eyes against the chill. He didn't because she had to see the truth in his eyes.

"All right." Her voice was tentative. "But don't betray me. I couldn't live with that again."

"I won't," he said, vowing he would never again take advantage of her trust. Nor would he let anything or anyone hurt her, not as long as he was alive to stop it.

"Let's go."

"How far away is it?"

"About twenty miles on Highway Eighty-Nine."

"Kelly, do you want some breakfast before we leave?"

"My stomach's so queasy, I couldn't hold it down. I want this to be over. Give me a minute to get ready and we can go."

He watched her walk out of the kitchen. He knew that after today, he would never see her again.

***

In the cab of the black pick-up truck, Nickels sipped coffee from a thermos. His phone rang. He placed the thermos between his legs and reached for it. "Yeah."

"The girl's time is up. Grab her and make her tell you where she hid the damn flash drive. Then do whatever you want before you kill her. If the man is with her, get rid of him too. Be careful. He's a tough bastard and he'll fight you to the death. Take him out first."

"It will cost more," Nickels said as he screwed the plastic lid back on the thermos.

"How much?"

"I'm easy. Let's say the same you're paying for the girl."

"You receive your money when I have the drive and I want to see the bodies." The phone disconnected.

The asshole didn't trust him or the bloodthirsty jerk probably wanted to shoot a few bullets into their bodies for his amusement.

Nickels' nerves flared. His hands itched. He took off the signet ring and scratched the reddened blisters that had formed under the ring.

221

A rush of adrenaline pulsed through his veins. He'd finally get to do his job and go back to his homeland.

***

The morning sun faded, turning the day gunmetal gray. Kelly watched the Sierra Nevada winds come in angry gusts to shake the trees. Moisture filled the air and it was only a matter of time before it snowed.

The tires gripped the narrow winding road that was Highway Eighty-Nine. She gave Brick directions to the Thumb Dumb house. The turn-off was near D.L. Bliss State Park and Emerald Bay, on the hillside away from the water.

From the car's window, she looked out at the inspiring view of Lake Tahoe.

How had her life come to this desperate point? In her desire to do good for Ted Simmons, she broke the rules by stealing from Johnny. *So, it is true no good deed goes unpunished.*

A blast of wind hit the vehicle and Brick jerked the steering wheel to keep the car on the right side of the road.

A snowflake hit the windshield. She stared as another one floated and landed on the hood, then more. *Snow at this time of year.*

She was reminded of the sunny day she, her sister, and their parents drove on this road to the Thumb Dumb House. It had been one of the last days they were all together.

The death of her parents had taught her how tenuous life could be. After they were gone, she had forced herself to go on living, determined to have a more exciting life than the boring one her parents had led. Without caring about the result, she'd taken any dare, if it meant she'd experience the exhilaration of life and proved she was

222

alive. Now the consequences of those actions had come home to roost.

If only she'd realized that her choices could spill over and put Carrie in danger too. If she had, different choices might have been made. She hadn't considered anyone but herself. *Damn.*

It didn't matter now. She couldn't change anything. Yet, the thought that she'd hurt Carrie and Brick, the two people she loved most, sent a jab of misery through her.

"Are you okay?"

"I have a sense of foreboding." She exhaled and rubbed her temples. "I can't shake it."

"After the last few days you've had, I'm not surprised. Don't worry. Soon, it'll be over." Brick glanced at her and then back to the road. "How much further?"

"A mile or two, I think. On the right side, there's a graveled lane."

"Good."

A myriad of emotions swirled in her. After the berating, she gave Brick yesterday, helping her. If only she hadn't said she detested him. She watched his profile, love for him beating in her chest. It didn't matter. It was too late. There was so much pain between them. Even if she lived, the chance of a relationship was gone.

"There hasn't been another vehicle on the road for miles. Now a pick-up truck is following us. The truck's holding its distance. Whether I slow down or speed up, the truck maintains the same distance between us," he said.

She started to turn around.

"Don't look. I don't want the driver to know we're on to him."

"Sorry." Her back tightened with anxiety. Was the truck following them or was it just a tourist on his way to his next destination?

As the snow increased, visibility decreased. She almost didn't see the lane. "There on the right," she yelled.

Brick swerved and quickly pulled off the highway onto a narrow path, stopped and waited. The truck following them sped by the turnoff without slowing.

"He wasn't following us." Relieved, she sighed and sat back.

Brick drove up the sideroad. The snow continued and the tires slipped on the slush. "Without chains, the car can't go any further." He turned off the engine. "We'll have to walk the rest of the way."

She jumped out of the car and followed him. The running shoes she wore weren't designed for this kind of weather. The wet snow soaked into the fabric of her runners and her feet became numb from the cold. She slid on the ice as she walked. Her warm breath mingled with the flakes and she tried to keep her balance.

They hiked in silence. An impatient expression spread over Brick's features.

"I didn't think it was so far." Her chest heaved with effort at the high altitude. "Sorry, I'm so slow. I guess I'm not used to this elevation anymore."

"Too many years at sea level."

"Yeah." She brushed snow from her eyes and squinted to see Brick just ahead of her.

Only the sounds of their labored breathing broke the silence as they reached the top of a knoll. A pine and granite mansion appeared before them, looming like a dark shadow in the flurry of white.

She prayed the flash drive was still where Carrie had hidden it.

"It must have been a grand house in its day." Brick rubbed his right knee, then stood and took a deep breath.

"It was beautiful when I was a kid. I thought of it as my very own castle."

"Let's grab the jump drive and get out of here."

When they got there, snow covered the granite stairs to the mansion's porch. She stepped carefully.

Brick pushed on the impressive oak-paneled front doors. One squeaked open. Motioning for her to wait, he entered the house alone.

Her sense of foreboding increased and she trembled, not only from the cold but from fear. She paced in front of the double doors of the old mansion. *Why was Brick taking so long?* She listened but couldn't hear any sounds coming from inside the house.

Her hand was on the metal door handle ready to turn it when she heard him shout, "It's okay. Come in."

In the grand foyer, a massive wooden staircase curved up to the second floor. Covered in dust, it didn't look as if anyone had used the stairs recently.

She listened for any sound that could help her find Brick. She entered a room that jutted off the entrance. It had no furniture and no Brick. She went back into the foyer.

"Where are you?"

"At the back of the house."

She followed the sound of his voice and entered a room dominated by floor-to-ceiling mahogany bookcases. The shelves were empty. She glanced from the bookcases to a beautifully carved support beam that held up the library's loft. It was also empty of books. "What a magnificent room. I can only imagine the volumes that must have lined the selves back in the day."

"Yeah, a few first additions, I bet." Brick leaned against the imposing granite mantle of the fireplace.

There had been a recent fire and embers glowed in the grate. The smell of burnt ashes and stale beer filled the room. "Smells like someone had a party." She wrinkled her nose. "I wonder who started the fire."

"Most likely local teens." He stood away from the fireplace. "I didn't find anyone in the house, but there are plenty of empty beer cans and bottles strewn around."

"I wish there was still a roaring fire." She stomped the ice from her shoes and shook the snow from her fleece top.

"Take my jacket."

"No. You need it."

"Take it." He took it off and put it over her shoulders.

"Thanks." She rolled up the long sleeves and put her arms in the jacket, still warm from his body heat. Sadness that she'd never know the feel of his arms around her again shot through her.

"Let's find the damned flash drive and leave before the storm gets worse," Brick said.

"Good idea."

She whirled toward the sound of a stranger's voice and faced the intruder who had burst into her house. A large man filled the doorway, a sinister smile on his lips, and a nine-millimeter pistol in his hand.

Chapter 26

The signet ring was still on the man's finger. Now Kelly knew the initial "N" on the ring stood for Nickels. She froze and her eyes focused on the weapon pointed at her chest.

"Get the flash drive."

"No." The word barely squeezed from her tightened throat.

"Do it."

His gun didn't waver from her. She was going to die and never get a chance to tell Brick she still loved him or ask for his forgiveness for all the horrible things she'd said to him.

"Move, bitch."

Brick cleared his throat.

Nickels spun toward him. "Take your weapon out of the holster. Put it on the floor and kick it to me or I'll kill the girl where she stands."

Adrenaline shot through her and her heart beat erratically.

"If you kill her, you'll never discover where the drive is."

How could he sound so relaxed?

"I can shoot both of you and search the place afterward."

Unbidden thoughts of Agent Simmons lying dead on the garage floor of the bungalow, his blood draining from his body, sparked in her mind. Her heart thumped and her knees started to buckle.

"I said drop the gun," Nickels demanded.

"Don't." She watched him take his firearm from his holster. "No."

He kicked it toward Nickels.

The guy grabbed her arm. "Pick it up."

Brick lunged at Nickels, sending a disabling blow to the man's solar plexus. He grunted and grabbed his rib cage, releasing her.

Brick knocked the revolver from the man's hand. It went flying across the room.

He twisted the thug's arm behind him and held it.

She gasped as he slammed Nickels' face into a wall and gripped the man's throat. "Who hired you?"

She saw him give Nickels just enough air to speak.

The man coughed but didn't answer.

"If you want to live, talk now. Who hired you?"

As Nickels opened his mouth to speak, a shot rang out. His eyes widened and blood dripped from a hole in his forehead. He dropped to the floor.

A tall stranger, with light brown hair, fierce eyes, and dressed in black jeans and a tan windbreaker, stood in the room. The average-looking man had just been murdered in cold blood. He stood with both hands still on his weapon, positioned to shoot again.

"Don! Are you crazy? Nickels was about to talk."

"No buddy, he was about to kill you."

She had trouble processing what was happening. Brick's boss was pointing a pistol at him.

"The man was under my control."

"No. He was going to shoot you." Don waved his pistol and smiled.

"You sent him," Brick gasped. "He was bought and paid for by you."

His supervisor didn't deny it.

Rage shone in Brick's expression. "He's your man. It all makes sense now. You always called me late at night or on the weekends and said not to alert the CIA."

His boss shrugged.

"There was no case, no file on Kelly. It was all a lie. The FBI didn't want her. You did."

His boss remained silent.

"It was a ruse to get me to use Kelly and find what you wanted. You knew she'd taken it. It was your only chance to retrieve it. You even sent the thugs to her house, so I'd stay and protect her, giving you a conduit to her."

"I didn't have to put a tracer on her car. You were my tracer and, like the good agent you are, you kept me informed of all your moves." Don smiled.

"And the information I sent to the FBI never went further than your desk." Bitterness crept into Brick's voice. "It was you, sending us out to find the guidance system.t, to help you turn against the United States for a buck."

"I warned you to watch your back."

"Don't do this. Not against your own country!"

"Mr. Kim Yi Jun is at Johnny Vega's penthouse waiting for the plans. Look buddy, the North Koreans won't use the guidance system. They could send a missile to Alaska or anywhere in the US right now, but they don't. The long-range guidance system will give them more accuracy and power at the negotiating table. If I make a few dollars on the deal, why not?"

"You're betraying your country. No matter what you tell yourself, that is what you're doing."

"You're an idealist, Brick. Your family's rich. You've never had to worry about how to pay your bills. Never had to face your kids and tell them there wasn't enough money."

"Don't use your kids as an excuse. I know them. They deserve better."

"Shut up!" Don stepped closer. "I didn't want you involved in this, but I didn't have a choice. Blame Kelly. If she hadn't stolen Johnny's flash drive, none of this would have happened."

"Yeah, you could've sold the system and no one would have been the wiser. How many copies were you going to make and sell?"

"With one impulsive act, the girl nearly destroyed all my years of planning." Don moved a step away from Brick. "I had to find her. Then I got an idea. You used to be engaged to her sister. I knew when you saw Kelly hurt and in trouble, you wouldn't leave her. You'd do anything to help. That's the kind of guard dog you are."

Kelly gasped.

"Just like a hound on the hunt, you didn't stop until you found the drive. Thanks. I couldn't have located it without you. You're good, but you've always been too damned trusting." Don laughed.

"And Ted Simmons, was he a good and trusting agent?"

"Ted was a hell of a nice guy. Too bad he stumbled upon information he wasn't supposed to have. I couldn't let him live. I'd come too far. I was too close to succeeding."

"You bastard!" Brick said through tightened teeth.

"I didn't kill him. He did." Don pointed to Nickels, dead on the floor.

"That makes it okay. Your hands are clean?"

His boss shrugged again.

"You had my house ransacked and nearly killed Amanda," Kelly screamed.

He looked as if he'd forgotten she was there.

"Hey, none of this is personal. I only did what I had to do."

"So here we are, just a couple of buddies, trying to get by?" Brick's blue eyes darkened to sapphire and then narrowed.

"I'm going to get the plan one way or the other. You might as well give it to me." He brought his pistol back into firing position, again pointing it at Brick.

Kelly rushed Don, hitting him with all her strength. He knocked her to the floor as he fired his weapon at Brick. Still, she'd pushed him hard enough to put off his aim and he missed hitting Brick square in the chest. Instead, the bullet tore through his left shoulder.

Before he could fire again, Brick tackled him. Intertwined, they rolled on the floor, a trail of Brick's blood left in their wake.

She saw him grimace. Despite the pain, he held onto his superior with his left hand and punched him with his right. His strength had to be draining with every drop of blood he lost. How much longer could he hold on to his boss? She loved Brick and if he died... She had to stop that thought. With Brick gone, she'd be at Don's mercy.

The room was silent except for the grunts of the two men. Still on the floor after being knocked down, she struggled to fill her lungs with air. The nine-millimeter weapon was on the floor about fifteen feet in front of her. The men rolled toward the fireplace and away from the gun. Intent on their own battle, they paid no attention to her.

She fought to breathe and crawled toward the pistol. When she reached it, the metal felt cold in her hands.

Just then, Don grabbed a log near the hearth and hit Brick in the head. Brick's eyes widened and then closed. Dead still, blood oozed from both his head wound and the bullet wound in his shoulder, and a trail of red slowly spilled onto the dusty oak floor.

With the log still in his hand, he raised his arm to hit Brick again.

"Stop or I will shoot!" She held the gun with both hands and pointed the nine-millimeter pistol at him. The weapon shook in her hands.

Don spun toward her as a smile formed on his thin lips. He took a step toward her.

"Stop!"

He froze and scanned her.

The pistol was her equalizer, but it was getting heavy. She fought to keep it level. Don was stockier than Brick and almost as tall as his six foot three inches. If the man came any closer, he'd grab her and wrestle the handgun away from her. She wouldn't be able to stop him.

Their eyes met. A chill crawled slowly up her spine. She tried to keep her fear from showing in her expression.

He shifted his position.

"Take a step and it'll be your last." Her voice sounded surprisingly strong. But her hands continued to tremble. She aimed the gun at his chest.

"You won't shoot me. You're a sweet kid. I know all about you. Killing's not in your nature." He smiled again but the log he'd used to hit Brick was still in his hand, ready to strike her. "You don't want to shoot me."

"A few days ago, you'd have been right. You've taught me to hate. I think of Ted and all the other hateful things you've done—I learn quickly. I could kill you and not miss a heartbeat."

His smile disappeared. "Brick needs you. He could bleed to death while we're talking. Give me what I want and I'll let you help him."

Terrified he might be telling the truth, she quickly glanced at Brick. He still hadn't moved. Hate for Don filled her. "On second thought, twitch, blink, raise an eyebrow so I *can* shoot you!"

"If he dies it will be your fault. You let him bleed to death."

"Damn, you!" Her voice cracked. "Just shut the hell up!"

Watching his predatory eyes, she kept the gun pointed at his heart. Still wearing Brick's jacket, with her left hand she felt in the jacket pocket. It was a relief to find his handcuffs were still there.

The ornately carved support beam that held up the library's loft caught her eye.

"Go to the support post." She tilted her head in the direction of the beam. "And put your arms around it."

Don didn't move, didn't even blink.

"Walk to the damned beam. Do it, or I'll shoot you where you stand!"

His eyes widened and then he slowly took a step. When he stood near it, he stopped.

"Do what I told you to do," she demanded.

"Make me." His expression hardened.

"I'll shoot you."

"Kelly, there's no way I will do what you ask." He grinned. "You're not going to shoot me. Give me the gun or I'll break your arm and take it."

233

Her muscles cried out in pain from holding the pistol out in front of her. She fought to stop her hands from quivering. He spoke the truth. She'd never shot a gun before. Could her first shot be one that killed a man, even one as despicable as Don? Still, if she didn't, she and Brick would die.

"I can see you won't be able to hold it much longer."

Shit. He was smiling again.

Brick moaned.

Thank God. He was alive. She forced her eyes to remain on Don. But more than anything else she wanted to go to Brick.

"He needs you. Give me the weapon and you can help him."

For half a second, she glanced at Brick. Don lunged for her. She pulled the trigger and he dropped to his knees, a look of astonishment on his face.

"I'm bleeding!"

Nausea rose in her throat. Unable to kill him, she'd aimed at his thigh. She stood ready to shoot again if he tried to move toward her.

He flushed with anger and struggled to stand, groaned, and then fell on his face.

She swallowed hard as her stomach retched.

Don sat up next to the beam, holding his wounded leg, blood seeping through his fingers.

She watched, hating him for all he had done. "Put your arms around the beam, or I'll shoot you again," she said, her voice firm.

"The hell, I'll bleed to death."

Brick moaned again.

"Do it!"

Without another word, he wrapped his arms around the post. She slipped the handcuffs around his wrist, just as Brick had done to Amanda's boyfriend.

How badly was Brick bleeding? She glanced in his direction.

She dropped the gun and ran to Brick. "Are you all right?"

His eyes gradually opened. "Get the drive," he said, his voice sounding surprisingly normal.

"You're hurt!"

"Just do it."

"I've got to stop the bleeding." She took off the jacket he'd given her, then tore off the fleece she was wearing under the jacket, leaving only her cotton T-shirt. She tied the fleece tightly around his shoulder.

"That's the best I can do for a bandage." A small red circle appeared on the pale pink fabric.

He rolled to his uninjured side and pushed to a sitting position. "Let's finish the job and get out of here."

"Wait a minute to be sure the blood has stopped."

"Where is it?"

"In the kitchen."

They entered the nineteen fifties kitchen. It was empty except for an old white refrigerator and a gas range. She prayed, then opened the oven door of the old gas-burning stove. In the dark oven, it was hard to see. Wishing she had a flashlight, she pulled out the metal shelves and ran her hand around the inside of the oven. She was about to stop, but in the far-left corner, her hand felt something.

"It's here." She wrapped her fingers tightly around the flash drive.

"Thank God." He grimaced, still cradling his left arm. "We'll burn it in the fireplace."

"Good." She glanced up at him and hoped her tears of relief didn't show on her face.

Back in the library, the fire in the pit had dwindled.

He stoked the glowing embers, then threw twigs and a small log into the fireplace. "It'll take a minute to catch fire."

She faced the granite fireplace watching the flames begin to rise. Heat spilled out into the room. The cold fear that had pulsed through her the last few days, started to diminish.

"The fire's hot enough, give me the drive," Brick put out his hand.

"I'll take that."

She spun around to see Johnny Vega in the doorway. His revolver was aimed at Brick.

Still handcuffed to the beam, Don sat up and smiled. "About time you got here. She shot me."

"This whole disaster is your fault." Johnny fired his firearm.

She screamed as Don slumped against the beam.

"Kelly, hand it to me or you're next." He waved the handgun at her.

The gruffness of Johnny's voice was all too familiar. She cringed.

"If you don't give it to me, I'm going to kill you. But first I'll beat the shit out of you."

She glanced at the fireplace. Could she throw it into the fire from where she stood before he could shoot her?

"Do you want to live or die, Kell? It's up to you." Johnny glared at her.

"Brick, what should I do?"

"Give it to him."

"But I…"

"It's all right. It's not worth you dying."

Shattered Rules

She held the flash drive out to Johnny. When he grabbed to get the drive, she dropped it.

As it landed on the floor, Brick dove at Johnny, hitting Vega with such force the pistol flew from his hand. They scrambled for it. Johnny grasped the pistol first. But before he could discharge the weapon, Brick sent a solid jab to the guy's abdomen, then a punch to his jaw. Johnny's head snapped backward and he dropped to the floor, motionless.

With the pistol in his left hand, Brick used his right hand to feel for Vega's carotid artery. He shook his head. "No use, he is done for. Vega's neck is broken."

She gasped.

Brick snatched the drive from the floor and carried it to the fireplace. With a hatchet, that lay next to the pile of wood, he smashed it.

"Let's do this before anyone else shows up," Brick said, his voice raw with pain.

"Oh God, what a thought."

He threw the pieces into the roaring fire. The flames flared higher but gave no extra warmth.

Soon the pieces disappeared into the red coals and mixed with the aroma of burning pine. The melting blobs, almost indiscernible from the other embers in the fire, continued to burn. He tossed another log on the fire.

Kelly watched a line of blood run down Brick's arm to his hand, and then drip onto the worn floorboards. He bent his elbow, brought the wounded arm up, and held it against his torso. His eyes didn't leave the fireplace and an undecipherable expression branded his face.

She flinched when Brick finally kneeled next to Don and checked for signs of life.

Brick's shoulders slumped. "Gone." He struggled to stand and returned to face the fire, silent and valiant.

Once again, he'd been betrayed by a friend. She wanted to comfort him but didn't know how. Her throat closed with emotion. Tears burned in her eyes. She brushed them away. He wouldn't want to see her cry.

Regret for the way she'd treated him shook her. He'd protected her, willing to give his life. All the terrible things she'd said to him came to haunt her, sending a shard of contrition. Even greater was her remorse for all that she'd done and the sorrow for the rules she'd shattered.

"I don't like the darkening sky."

She glanced out the window.

"Looks like the storm might get worse." He picked up the guns, putting his pistol into his shoulder holster and the others in the pockets of the jacket she was still wearing. "We need to leave."

"What about them?" She turned away and didn't look at the men lying still on the library floor.

He pulled his cell phone from his pocket. "No service. When we get back to Tahoe City, I'll call and have the FBI send a team to take care of things. With this snowstorm, no one will get here before the Bureau."

Cradling his left arm close to his body, .Brick walked slowly out of the room,

She followed him outside.

As if to cleanse the area, snow fell hard in the Sierra Nevada Mountain range. Standing by his side on the porch, she viewed the silent storm.

"Kelly, we'll have a lot of questions to answer when we get back. I'll stay with you and we'll do it together."

"Brick, I'm sorry for not telling you what Agent Simmons and I were doing. I feel terrible about everything." She swallowed hard to keep from crying. "I have so much regret."

He put his uninjured arm around her. "We all have remorse." He took a slow breath. "That's not important now. The plan for the missile guidance system has been destroyed." He pulled her closer. "Against the odds, we did it. We're good together. Of course, the US will have to watch North Korea. Eternal vigilance will be needed to keep the peace."

She leaned her head on his broad chest and listened to his rapidly beating heart. "You mean everything to me, Brick."

"I love you, Kelly. I want you by my side for the rest of my life."

She gazed up at him. "I want that more than anything else in the world."

He bent down and laid a gentle kiss on her waiting lips. "Forever," he promised.

"Always," she agreed.

Together they turned their backs on the mansion and its horror and walked toward their future.

*****

Thank you for reading this book, if you enjoyed it, please leave a positive review on Amazon, Bookbub.com, Allauthor.com, or Goodreads.com

Reviews don't have to be long, a sentence or two will do. They are helpful to both the reader and the author.

About the Author

Reggi Allder writes suspense and contemporary novels. Her characters must overcome obstacles in both genres, as in real life. The males are strong, though they may be wounded. The women are determined to change their lives to manage their future. They fight to discover a hidden strength and work toward a lifelong goal.

Reggi Allder

She studied creative writing and screenwriting at the University of California at Los Angeles (UCLA). Besides the standalone books, she writes The Sierra Creek Series, Book One Her Country Heart, and the Dangerous Series, Book One Dangerous Web. She has also contributed to cookbooks and has written children's stories.

Reggi enjoys hearing from readers.ReggiAllder.com Follow her on, Bookbub.com, and Facebook.

Please read on:
Dangerous Web by Reggi Allder.

Excerpt:

As the country road made a sharp turn to the left, the cabin came into view surrounded by ponderosa pine. The house stood strong, but weathered and unwelcoming. The perennials she'd planted in the front yard lay lifeless, as dead as her relationship with her husband. Seeing them sent a shard of pain through her. *Don't think about what might have been.*

Why had it taken so long to understand her husband was gone? Until now, she'd held out hope. In the waning daylight, she stared at their vacation home. It was finally time to accept the truth. The marriage was over.

She parked, turned off the engine, and let out a single sob. *Stop. No crying. You've done more than enough in the last two years.*

The wooden stairs squeaked as she climbed to the large front deck. With shaking fingers, she held the cold metal door key in her hand.

"Miss."

She jumped at the sound of the male voice and glanced at a forty-something man dressed in jeans and a khaki shirt. He wiped his brow before putting a black and orange baseball cap on his brown shaggy hair.

"Yes."

"I can finish weeding the backyard garden, but I'll have to come back later and get the fallen tree behind the house. Got to get a bigger truck if you want the whole tree cut up and taken away." He rubbed the stubble on his chin. "Or I can leave the wood for your fireplace."

A chill ran down her back. It wasn't as if he said anything menacing, but she hadn't sent for a gardener. "There must be a mistake. I never called for a gardener."

"I've been coming here for two years."

"Impossible. I—two years?"

He sniffed and rubbed his nose.

"Look mister, I own this place. I never ordered or paid you to do work in this garden."

"I wouldn't know. I only do what I'm told." He pulled a kerchief from his back pocket and rubbed his neck. "You got a branch in the backyard, almost broke a window. If it's not cut and pulled away from there today, you could end up in trouble. A storm is coming." He sniffed again.

"But I..."

"Lady, I was sent to do a job. You got a problem, call my boss. I'll move the branch from the window before the glass gets broke. You can take up the bill with the company. You'll be glad I was here when the rain and thunder come tonight."

"Okay—if it'll prevent the window from shattering, but..."

He walked toward a nearby truck, apparently finished with the conversation.

241

Stunned, she stood on the deck trying to make sense of who would pay for the yard work.

She glanced at the pickup's door. "Sierra Gardeners." Later, she'd call and find out who was shelling out money for the job.

Carrying a dustpan and broom in one hand, and her keys and purse in the other, she put everything down and pulled her phone from her jacket pocket.

No signal, she should have understood being so rural there wouldn't be a cell tower nearby.

As she headed for the front door, the sound of a chainsaw broke through the quiet. The door squeaked open when she turned the key in the cabin's lock. The knotty pine walls had darkened, but the handmade sofa and chairs were still where she'd placed them. The turquoise and sage green upholstery, chosen so carefully, now appeared to mock her. "Our love nest," she whispered to no one.

The smell of smoke wafted toward her. She'd expected mildew or dust, but never a burning oak log in the brick fireplace. Had the gardener started a fire? Would he have the nerve to come into the house? She set her purse and keys on the entry table. Coffee? She took another whiff of the indoor air and smelled freshly brewed coffee.

A chill jogged down her back. "Hello. Is anyone here?"

Silence.

In the kitchen, a French press coffeemaker sat on the Formica table. She touched it. *Hot.* It had to be the gardener. After all, he hadn't expected her. Being far from anyone, it might be his routine to make himself at home. She shook away her fear.

Shattered Rules

To be sure she was alone, she'd check the rooms. The first bedroom was empty. She froze at the door of the master bedroom. Her wedding night played in her mind. *Honey, don't be shy.* Her husband had coxed her. *You're beautiful. I love you, Emmy. Come to me.*

"No." She wouldn't relive the night, not now, not ever.

The pine floorboards squeaked as she entered the bedroom and flicked on the overhead light to illuminate the dark wood walls. The green and blue landscape she had found in an antique store, still hungover whitewashed pine bed. She pushed back a curtain. Men's shirts hung on the wooden rod in the cedar-clad closet. A duffel bag sat on the floor.

A squatter's living here. Oh God. No, wait. Would a squatter hang up his shirts?

She ran from the room to the backyard. Waving her hands to get the gardener's attention, she yelled, "Are you living in the cabin?"

Dangerous Web by Reggi Allder

Books by Reggi Allder

Suspense
Dangerous Series:
Dangerous Web
Dangerous Denial
Dangerous Money
Dangerous Moves
Suspense
Shattered Rules

Contemporary
Sierra Creek Series
Her Country Heart
His Country Heart
Our Country Heart
My Country Heart
Her Country Heart Christmas Edition

Historical
With Glowing Hearts

Coming Next
Dangerous Sisters